RETURN OF
THE MUMMY

Goosebumps®

RETURN OF THE MUMMY

R.L. STINE

SCHOLASTIC INC.

NEW YORK TORONTO LONDON AUCKLAND
SYDNEY MEXICO CITY NEW DELHI HONG KONG

No part of this publication may be reproduced, stored in a retrieval system, or transmitted in any form or by any means, electronic, mechanical, photocopying, recording, or otherwise, without written permission of the publisher. For information regarding permission, write to Scholastic Inc., Attention: Permissions Department, 557 Broadway, New York, NY 10012.

ISBN 978-0-545-17794-8

Goosebumps book series created by Parachute Press, Inc.
Copyright © 1994 by Scholastic Inc.

All rights reserved. Published by Scholastic Inc., *Publishers since 1920*.
SCHOLASTIC, GOOSEBUMPS, GOOSEBUMPS HORRORLAND, and associated logos are trademarks and/or registered trademarks of Scholastic Inc.

12 11 10 9 8 7 6 5   16/0

Printed in the U.S.A.   40
First printing, December 2010

"Behind the Screams" bonus material by Gabrielle S. Balkan

"Gabe, we will be landing soon," the stewardess told me, leaning over the seat. "Will someone be meeting you at the airport?"

"Yes. Probably an ancient Egyptian pharaoh," I told her. "Or maybe a disgusting, decaying mummy."

She narrowed her eyes at me. "No. Really," she insisted. "Who will be meeting you in Cairo?"

"My Uncle Ben," I replied. "But he likes to play practical jokes. Sometimes he dresses in weird costumes and tries to scare me."

"You told me that your uncle was a famous scientist," the stewardess said.

"He is," I replied. "But he's also weird."

She laughed. I liked her a lot. She had pretty blond hair. And I liked the way she always tilted her head to one side when she talked.

Her name was Nancy, and she had been very nice to me during the long flight to Egypt. She knew it was my first time flying all by myself.

1

She kept checking on me and asking me how I was doing. But she treated me like a grown-up. She didn't bring me one of those dumb connect-the-dots books or a plastic wings pin that they always give to kids on planes. And she kept slipping me extra bags of peanuts, even though she wasn't supposed to.

"Why are you visiting your uncle?" Nancy asked. "Just for fun?"

I nodded. "I did it last winter, too," I told her. "It was really awesome! But this year, Uncle Ben has been digging in an unexplored pyramid. He's discovered an ancient, sacred tomb. And he invited me to be with him when he opens it up."

She laughed and tilted her head a little more. "You have a good imagination, Gabe," she said. Then she turned away to answer a man's question.

I *do* have a good imagination. But I wasn't making that up.

My Uncle Ben Hassad is a famous archaeologist. He has been digging around in pyramids for lots of years. I've seen newspaper articles about him. And once he was in *National Geographic*.

Last Christmas, my entire family visited Cairo. My cousin Sari and I — she's Uncle Ben's daughter — had some amazing adventures down in the chambers of the Great Pyramid.

Sari will be there this summer, too, I remembered, staring out the plane window at the solid

2

blue sky. I wondered if maybe she would give me a break this time.

I like Sari, but she's so competitive! She always has to be the first, the strongest, the smartest, the best. She's the only thirteen-year-old girl I know who can turn eating breakfast into a contest!

"Flight attendants, prepare for landing," the pilot announced over the loudspeaker.

I sat up to get a better view out the window. As the plane lowered, I could see the city of Cairo beneath us. A slender blue ribbon curled through the city. That, I knew, was the Nile River.

The city stretched out from the river. Peering straight down, I could see tall glass skyscrapers and low domed temples. Where the city ended, the desert began. Yellow sand stretched to the horizon.

My stomach began to feel a little fluttery. The pyramids were somewhere out in that desert. And in a day or two, I would be climbing down into one of them, following my uncle into a tomb that hadn't been opened for thousands of years.

What would we find?

I pulled the little mummy hand from my shirt pocket and gazed down at it. It was so tiny—no bigger than a child's hand. I had bought it from a kid at a garage sale for two dollars. He said it was called a Summoner. He said it could summon ancient evil spirits.

It looked like a mummy hand. The fingers were wrapped in stained gauze bandages with a little black tar showing through.

I thought it was a fake, made of rubber or plastic. I mean, I never thought it was a real mummy hand.

But last year, the hand had saved all of our lives. The kid who sold it to me was right. It really did bring a bunch of mummies to life! It was *amazing*!

Of course my parents and my friends back home didn't believe my incredible story. And they didn't believe that the Summoner really worked. They said it was just a joke mummy hand made in some souvenir factory. Probably made in Taiwan.

But I carry it with me wherever I go. It is my good luck charm. I'm not very superstitious. I mean, I walk under ladders all the time. And my lucky number is thirteen.

But I really do believe that the little mummy hand will protect me.

The strange thing about the mummy hand is that it is always warm. It doesn't feel like plastic. It feels warm, like a real human hand.

Back home in Michigan, I had a major panic attack when Mom and Dad were packing my suitcase for the flight. I couldn't find the mummy hand. And, of course, there was *no way* I would go to Egypt without it!

4

I was so relieved when I finally found it. It was tucked into the back pocket of a crumpled-up pair of jeans.

Now, as the plane nosed down for a landing, I reached for the hand in the pocket of my T-shirt. I pulled it out—and gasped.

The hand was cold. Cold as ice!

Why had the mummy hand suddenly turned cold?

Was it some kind of a message? A warning?

Was I heading into danger?

I didn't have time to think about it. The plane rolled into the gate, and the passengers were scrambling to pull down their carry-on bags and push their way out of the plane.

I tucked the mummy hand into my jeans pocket, hoisted up my backpack, and headed to the front. I said good-bye to Nancy and thanked her for all the peanuts. Then I followed the others down the long covered ramp and into the airport.

So many people!

And they all seemed to be in a hurry. They were practically stepping over each other. Men in dark business suits. Women in loose, flowing robes, their faces covered by veils. Teenage girls in jeans and T-shirts. A group of dark, serious-looking men in silky white suits that looked like pajamas. A family with three little kids, all crying.

I had a sudden sinking feeling. How would I ever find Uncle Ben in this crowd?

My backpack began to feel very heavy. My eyes frantically searched back and forth. Strange voices surrounded me, all talking so loudly. No one was speaking English.

"Ow!" I cried out as I felt a sharp pain in my side.

I turned and realized that a woman had bumped me with her luggage cart.

Stay calm, Gabe, I instructed myself. *Just stay calm.*

Uncle Ben is here, looking for you. He'll find you. You just have to stay calm.

But what if he forgot? I asked myself. *What if he got mixed up about what day I was arriving? Or what if he got busy down in the pyramid and lost track of the time?*

I can be a real worrier if I put my mind to it.

And right now I was worrying enough for three people!

If Uncle Ben isn't here, I'll go to a phone and call him, I decided.

For sure.

I could just hear myself saying, "Operator, can I speak to my uncle at the pyramids, please?"

I don't think that would work too well.

I didn't have a phone number for Uncle Ben. I wasn't sure he even *had* a phone out where he was staying. All I knew was that he had been living in a tent somewhere near the pyramid where he was digging.

Gazing frantically around the crowded arrival area, I was just about to give in to total panic — when a large man came walking up to me.

I couldn't see his face. He wore a long white hooded robe. It's called a burnoose. And his face was buried inside the hood.

"Taxi?" he asked in a high, shrill voice. "Taxi? American taxi?"

I burst out laughing. "Uncle Ben!" I cried happily.

"Taxi? American taxi? Taxi ride?" he insisted.

"Uncle Ben! I'm so glad to see you!" I exclaimed. I threw my arms around his waist and gave him a big hug. Then, laughing at his stupid disguise, I reached up and pulled back his hood.

The man under the hood had a bald, shaved head and a heavy black mustache. He glared at me furiously.

I had never seen him before in my life.

"Gabe! Gabe! Over here!"

I heard a voice calling my name. Glancing past the angry man, I saw Uncle Ben and Sari. They were waving to me from in front of the reservations counter.

The man's face turned bright red, and he shouted something at me in Arabic. I was glad I couldn't understand him. He kept muttering as he pulled up the hood of his burnoose.

"Sorry about that!" I cried. Then I dodged past him and hurried to greet Uncle Ben and my cousin.

Uncle Ben shook my hand and said, "Welcome to Cairo, Gabe." He was wearing a loose-fitting white short-sleeved sport shirt and baggy chinos.

Sari wore faded denim cutoffs and a bright green tank top. She was already laughing at me. A bad start. "Was that a friend of yours?" she teased.

"I—I made a mistake," I confessed. I glanced back. The man was still scowling at me.

"Did you really think that was Daddy?" Sari demanded.

I mumbled a reply. Sari and I were the same age. But I saw that she was still an inch taller than me. She had let her black hair grow. It fell down her back in a single braid.

Her big dark eyes sparkled excitedly. She *loved* making fun of me.

I told them about my flight as we walked to the baggage area to get my suitcase. I told them how Nancy, the stewardess, kept slipping me bags of peanuts.

"I flew here last week," Sari told me. "The stewardess let *me* sit in first class. Did you know you can have an ice cream sundae in first class?"

No, I didn't know that. I could see that Sari hadn't changed a bit.

She goes to a boarding school in Chicago since Uncle Ben has been spending all of his time in Egypt. Of course she gets straight A's. And she's a champion skier and tennis player.

Sometimes I feel a little sorry for her. Her mom died when Sari was five. And Sari only gets to see her dad on holidays and during the summer.

But as we waited for my suitcase to come out on the conveyor belt, I wasn't feeling sorry for her at all. She was busy bragging about how this pyramid was twice as big as the one I'd been in last year. And how she'd already been down in it several times, and how she'd take me on a tour— if I wasn't too afraid.

Finally, my bulging blue suitcase appeared. I lugged it off the conveyor and dropped it at my feet. It weighed a ton!

I tried to lift it, but I could barely budge it.

Sari pushed me out of the way. "Let *me* get that," she insisted. She grabbed the handle, raised the suitcase off the floor, and started off with it.

"Hey!" I called after her. What a show-off!

Uncle Ben grinned at me. "I think Sari has been working out," he said. He put a hand on my shoulder and led me toward the glass doors. "Let's get to the Jeep."

We loaded the suitcase into the back of the Jeep, then headed toward the city. "It's been sweltering hot during the day," Uncle Ben told me, mopping his broad forehead with a handkerchief. "And then cool at night."

Traffic crawled on the narrow street. Horns honked constantly. Drivers kept their horns going whether they moved or stopped. The noise was deafening.

"We're not stopping in Cairo," Uncle Ben explained. "We're going straight to the pyramid at al-Jizah. We're all living in tents out there so we can be close to our work."

11

"I hope you brought bug spray," Sari complained. "The mosquitoes are as big as frogs!"

"Don't exaggerate," Uncle Ben scolded. "Gabe isn't afraid of a few mosquitoes—are you?"

"No way," I replied quietly.

"How about scorpions?" Sari demanded.

The traffic grew lighter as we left the city behind and headed into the desert. The yellow sand gleamed under the hot afternoon sun. Waves of heat rose up in front of us as the Jeep bumped over the narrow two-lane road.

Before long, a pyramid came into view. Behind the waves of heat off the desert floor, it looked like a wavering mirage. It didn't seem real.

As I stared out at it, my throat tightened with excitement. I had seen the pyramids last Christmas. But it was still a thrilling sight.

"I can't believe the pyramids are thousands of years old!" I exclaimed.

"Yeah. That's even older than *me*!" Uncle Ben joked. His expression turned serious. "It fills me with pride every time I see them, Gabe," he admitted. "To think that our ancient ancestors were smart enough and skilled enough to build these marvels."

Uncle Ben was right. I guess the pyramids have special meaning for me since my family is Egyptian. Both sets of my grandparents came from Egypt. They moved to the United States around 1930. My mom and dad were born in Michigan.

I think of myself as a typical American kid. But there's still something exciting about visiting the country where your ancestors came from.

As we drove nearer, the pyramid appeared to rise up in front of us. Its shadow formed a long blue triangle over the yellow sand.

Cars and tour buses jammed a small parking lot. I could see a row of saddled camels tethered on one side of the lot. A crowd of tourists stretched across the sand, gazing up at the pyramid, snapping photographs, chatting noisily and pointing.

Uncle Ben turned the Jeep onto a narrow side road, and we headed away from the crowd, toward the back of the pyramid. As we drove into the shade, the air suddenly felt cooler.

"I'd *kill* for an ice cream cone!" Sari wailed. "I've never been so hot in my life."

"Let's not talk about the heat," Uncle Ben replied, sweat dripping down his forehead into his bushy eyebrows. "Let's talk about how happy you are to see your father after so many months."

Sari groaned. "I'd be happier to see you if you were carrying an ice cream cone."

Uncle Ben laughed.

A khaki-uniformed guard stepped in front of the Jeep. Uncle Ben held up a blue ID card. The guard waved us past.

As we followed the road behind the pyramid, a row of low white canvas tents came into view. "Welcome to the Pyramid Hilton!" Uncle Ben joked. "That's our luxury suite over there." He pointed to the nearest tent.

"It's pretty comfortable," he said, parking the Jeep beside the tent. "But the room service is lousy."

"And you have to watch out for scorpions," Sari warned.

She'd say *anything* to try to scare me.

We unloaded my suitcase. Then Uncle Ben led us up to the base of the pyramid.

A camera crew was packing up its equipment. A young man, covered in dust, climbed out of a low entrance dug into one of the limestone squares. He waved to my uncle, then hurried toward the tents.

"One of my people," Uncle Ben muttered. He motioned toward the pyramid. "Well, here you are, Gabe. A long way from Michigan, huh?"

I nodded. "It's amazing," I told him, shielding my eyes to gaze up to the top. "I forgot how much bigger the pyramids look in person."

"Tomorrow I'll take you both down to the tomb," Uncle Ben promised. "You've come at just the right time. We've been digging for months and months. And at long last, we are about to break the seal and enter the tomb itself."

"Wow!" I exclaimed. I wanted to be cool in front of Sari. But I couldn't help it. I was really excited.

"Guess you'll be really famous after you open the tomb, huh, Dad?" Sari asked. She swatted a fly on her arm. *"Ow!"*

"I'll be so famous, the flies will be afraid to bite you," Uncle Ben replied. "By the way, do you know what they called flies in ancient Egypt?"

Sari and I shook our heads no.

"I don't, either!" Uncle Ben said, grinning. One of his dumb jokes. He had an endless supply of them. His expression suddenly changed. "Oh. That reminds me. I have a present for you, Gabe."

"A present?"

"Now, where did I put it?" He dug both hands into the pockets of his baggy chinos.

As he searched, I saw something move behind him. A shadow over my uncle's shoulder, back at the low opening to the pyramid.

I squinted at it.

The shadow moved. A figure stepped out slowly.

At first I thought the sun was playing tricks on my eyes.

But as I squinted harder, I realized that I was seeing correctly.

The figure stepped out from the pyramid—its face was covered in worn, yellowed gauze. So were its arms. And its legs.

I opened my mouth to cry out—but my voice choked in my throat.

And as I struggled to alert my uncle, the mummy stiffly stretched out its arms and came staggering up behind him.

I saw Sari's eyes grow wide with fright. She let out a low gasp.

"Uncle Ben!" I finally managed to scream. "Turn around! It—it—!"

My uncle narrowed his eyes at me, confused.

The mummy staggered closer, its hands reaching out menacingly, about to grab the back of Uncle Ben's neck.

"A *mummy*!" I shrieked.

Uncle Ben spun around. He let out a startled cry. "It walks!" he shouted, pointing at the mummy with a trembling finger. He backed away as the mummy advanced. "It walks!"

"Ohhh." A strange moan escaped Sari's lips.

I turned and started to run.

But then the mummy burst out laughing.

It lowered its yellowed arms. "Boo!" it cried, and laughed again.

I turned and saw that Uncle Ben was laughing, too. His dark eyes sparkled gleefully.

"It walks! It walks!" he repeated, shaking his head. He put his arm around the mummy's shoulder.

I gaped at the two of them, my heart still pounding.

"This is John," Uncle Ben said, enjoying the joke he'd pulled on us. "He's been doing a TV commercial here. For some new kind of stickier bandage."

"Sticky Bird Bandages," John told us. "They're just what your mummy ordered!"

He and Uncle Ben enjoyed another good laugh at that. Then my uncle pointed to the camera crew, packing their equipment into a small van. "They finished for the day. But John agreed to hang around and help me scare you."

Sari rolled her eyes. "Nice try," she said dryly. "You'll have to do better than that, Daddy, to frighten me." And then she added, "Poor Gabe. Did you see his face? He was so freaked out! I thought he was going to spontaneously *combust* or something!"

Uncle Ben and John laughed.

"Hey—no way!" I insisted, feeling my face turn red.

How could Sari *say* that? When the mummy staggered out, I saw her gasp and back away. She was just as scared as I was!

"I heard you scream, too!" I told her. I didn't mean to sound so whiny.

"I just did that to help them scare you," Sari insisted. She tossed her long braid over her shoulder.

"I've got to run," John said, glancing at his wristwatch. "As soon as we get back to the hotel, I'm going to hit the pool. I may stay underwater for a week!" He gave us a wave of his bandaged hand and went jogging to the van.

Why hadn't I noticed that he was wearing a wristwatch?

I felt like a total dork. "That's it!" I cried angrily to my uncle. "I'm never falling for one of your dumb jokes again! Never!"

He grinned at me and winked. "Want to bet?"

"What about Gabe's present?" Sari asked. "What is it?"

Uncle Ben pulled something out of his pocket and held it up. A pendant on a string. Made of clear orange glass. It gleamed in the bright sunlight.

He handed it to me. I moved it in my hand, feeling its smoothness as I examined it. "What is it?" I asked him. "What kind of glass is this?"

"It isn't glass," he replied. "It's a clear stone called amber." He stepped closer to examine it along with me. "Hold it up and look inside the pendant."

I followed his instructions. I saw a large brown bug inside. "It looks like some kind of beetle," I said.

"It *is* a beetle," Uncle Ben said, squinting one eye to see it better. "It's an ancient beetle called a scarab. It was trapped in the amber three thousand years ago. As you can see, it's perfectly preserved."

"That's really gross," Sari commented, making a face. She slapped Uncle Ben on the back. "Great gift, Dad. A dead bug. Remind me not to let you do our Christmas shopping!"

Uncle Ben laughed. Then he turned back to me. "The scarab was very important to the ancient Egyptians," he said. "They believed that scarabs were a symbol of immortality."

I stared at the bug's dark shell, its six prickly legs, perfectly preserved.

"To keep a scarab meant immortality," my uncle continued. "But the bite of a scarab meant instant death."

"Weird," Sari muttered.

"It's great looking," I told him. "Is it really three thousand years old?"

He nodded. "Wear it around your neck, Gabe. Maybe it still has some of its ancient powers."

I slipped the pendant over my head and adjusted it under my T-shirt. The amber stone felt cool against my skin. "Thanks, Uncle Ben," I said. "It's a great present."

He mopped his sweaty forehead with a wadded-up handkerchief. "Let's go back to the tent and get something cold to drink," he said.

We took a few steps—and then stopped when we saw Sari's face.

Her entire body trembled. Her mouth dropped open as she pointed to my chest.

"Sari—what *is* it?" Uncle Ben cried.

"The s-scarab—" she stammered. "It . . . escaped! I saw it!" She pointed down. "It's there!"

"Huh?" I spun away from her and bent down to find the scarab.

"Ow!" I cried out when I felt a sharp stab of pain on the back of my leg.

And realized the scarab had bitten me.

As I gasped in alarm, Uncle Ben's words about the scarab rushed through my mind.

"To keep a scarab meant immortality. But the bite of a scarab meant instant death."

Instant death?

"Noooo!" I let out a howl and spun around.

And saw Sari hunched down on her knees. Grinning. Her hand outstretched.

And realized she had pinched my leg.

My heart still pounding, I grabbed the pendant and stared into the orange glassy stone. The scarab was still frozen inside, just as it had been for three thousand years.

"Aaaaaaaaygh!" I let out a howl of rage. I was mostly furious at myself.

Was I going to fall for every dumb joke Uncle Ben and Sari played on me this trip? If so, it was going to be a very long summer.

I had always liked my cousin. Except for the

times when she was being so competitive and so superior, we always got along really well.

But now I wanted to punch her. I wanted to say really nasty things to her.

But I couldn't think of anything nasty enough.

"That was really mean, Sari," I said glumly, tucking the pendant under my T-shirt.

"Yes, it was—*wasn't* it!" she replied, very pleased with herself.

That night, I lay on my back on my narrow cot, staring up at the low tent roof, listening. Listening to the brush of the wind against the tent door, the soft creak of the tent poles, the flap of the canvas.

I don't think I'd ever felt so alert.

Turning my head, I could see the pale glow of moonlight through a crack in the tent door. I could see blades of dried desert grass on the sand outside. I could see water stains on the tent wall over my bed.

I'll never get to sleep, I thought unhappily.

I pushed and punched the flat pillow for the twentieth time, trying to fluff it up. The harsh wool blanket felt scratchy against my chin.

I'd slept away from home before. But I'd always slept in a room of some kind. Not in the middle of a vast sandy desert in a tiny, flapping, creaking canvas tent.

I wasn't scared. My uncle lay snoring away in his cot a few feet across the tent.

I was just alert. Very, very alert.

So alert I could hear the swish of palm trees outside. And I could hear the low hum of car tires miles away on the narrow road.

And I heard the thudding of my heart when something wriggled on my chest.

I was so alert, I felt it instantly.

Just a tickle. A quick, light move.

It could only be one thing. The scarab moving inside the amber pendant.

No joke this time.

No joke. It moved.

I fumbled for the pendant in the dark, tossing down the blanket. I held it up to the moonlight. I could see the fat beetle in there, black in its orange prison.

"Did you move?" I whispered to it. "Did you wriggle your legs?"

I suddenly felt really stupid. Why was I whispering to a three-thousand-year-old insect? Why was I imagining that it was alive?

Annoyed with myself, I tucked the pendant back under my nightshirt.

I had no way of knowing how important that pendant would soon become to me.

I had no way of knowing that the pendant held a secret that would either save my life—or kill me.

The tent was already hot when I awoke the next morning. Bright yellow sunlight poured in through the open tent flap. Squinting against the light, I rubbed my eyes and stretched. Uncle Ben had already gone out.

My back ached. The little cot was so hard!

But I was too excited to worry about my back. I was going down into the pyramid this morning, to the entrance of an ancient tomb.

I pulled on a clean T-shirt and the jeans I'd worn the day before. I adjusted the scarab pendant under the T-shirt. Then I carefully tucked the little mummy hand into the back pocket of my jeans.

With the pendant and the mummy hand, I'm well protected, I told myself. *Nothing bad can happen this trip.*

I pulled a hairbrush through my thick black hair a few times, tugged my black-and-yellow Michigan Wolverines cap on. Then I hurried to the mess tent to get some breakfast.

The sun was floating above the palm trees in the distance. The yellow desert sand gleamed brightly. I took a deep breath of fresh air.

Yuck. There must be some camels nearby, I decided. The air wasn't exactly fresh.

I found Sari and Uncle Ben having their breakfast, seated at the end of the long table in the mess tent. Uncle Ben wore his usual baggy chinos and a short-sleeved white sport shirt with coffee stains down the front.

Sari had her long black hair pulled straight back in a ponytail. She wore a bright red tank top over white tennis shorts.

They greeted me as I entered the tent. I poured myself a glass of orange juice and, since I didn't see any Frosted Flakes, filled a bowl with raisin bran.

Three of Uncle Ben's workers were eating at the other end of the table. They were talking excitedly about their work. "We could go in today," I heard one of them say.

"It might take days to break the seal on the tomb door," a young woman replied.

I sat down next to Sari. "Tell me all about the tomb," I said to Uncle Ben. "Whose tomb is it? What's in there?"

He chuckled. "Let me say good morning before I launch into a lecture."

Sari leaned over my cereal bowl. "Hey, look—" she said, pointing. "I got a lot more raisins than you did!"

I *told* you she could turn breakfast into a contest.

"Well, I got more pulp in my orange juice," I replied.

It was just a joke, but she checked her juice glass to make sure.

Uncle Ben wiped his mouth with a paper napkin. He took a long sip of black coffee. "If I'm not mistaken," he began, "the tomb we have discovered here belonged to a prince. Actually, a cousin of King Tutankhamun."

"That's King Tut," Sari told me, interrupting.

"I know that!" I replied sharply.

"King Tut's tomb was discovered in 1922," Uncle Ben continued. "The vast burial chamber was filled with most of Tut's treasures. It was the most amazing archaeological discovery of its time." A smile crossed his face. "Until now."

"Do you think you've found something even more amazing?" I asked. I hadn't touched my cereal. I was too interested in my uncle's story.

He shrugged. "There's no way of knowing what's behind the tomb door until we open it, Gabe. But I have my fingers crossed. I believe we've found the burial chamber of Prince Khor-Ru. He was the king's cousin. And he was said to be as wealthy as the king."

"And do you think all of Prince Khor-Ru's crowns, and jewels, and belongings are buried with him?" Sari asked.

Uncle Ben took the last sip of coffee and slid the white mug across the table. "Who knows?" he replied. "There could be amazing treasures in there. Or it could be empty. Just an empty room."

"How could it be empty?" I demanded. "Why would there be an empty tomb in the pyramid?"

"Grave robbers," Uncle Ben replied, frowning. "Remember, Prince Khor-Ru was buried sometime around 1300 B.C. Over the centuries, thieves broke into the pyramids and robbed the treasures from many burial chambers."

He stood up and sighed. "We may have been digging for all these months only to find an empty room."

"No way!" I cried excitedly. "I'll bet we find the prince's mummy in there. And millions of dollars' worth of jewels!"

Uncle Ben smiled at me. "Enough talk," he said. "Finish your breakfast so we can go find out."

Sari and I followed Uncle Ben out of the tent. He waved to two young men who came out of the supply tent carrying digging equipment. Then he hurried over to talk to them.

Sari and I lingered behind. She turned to me, a serious expression on her face. "Hey, Gabe," she said softly, "sorry I've been such a pain."

"You? A pain?" I replied sarcastically.

She didn't laugh. "I'm kind of worried," she confessed. "About Daddy."

I glanced at Uncle Ben. He was slapping one of the young men on the back as he talked. His usually jolly self.

"Why are you worried?" I asked Sari. "Your dad is in a great mood."

"That's why I'm worried," Sari whispered. "He's so happy and excited. He really thinks this is going to be the discovery that makes him famous."

"So?" I demanded.

"So what if it turns out to be an empty room?" Sari replied, her dark eyes watching her father. "What if grave robbers did strip the place? Or what if it isn't that prince's tomb after all? What if Daddy breaks the seal, opens the door—and finds nothing but a dusty old room filled with snakes?"

She sighed. "Daddy will be heartbroken. Just heartbroken. He's counting on this so much, Gabe. I don't know if he'll be able to take the disappointment."

"Why look on the gloomy side?" I replied. "What if—"

I stopped because Uncle Ben was hurrying back to us. "Let's go down to the chamber," he said excitedly. "The workers think we are very close to uncovering the tomb entrance."

He put an arm on each of our shoulders and guided us to the pyramid.

As we stepped into the shade of the pyramid, the air grew cooler. The low entrance dug at the bottom of the back wall came into view. It was just big enough for us to enter one at a time. Peering into the narrow hole, I saw that the tunnel dropped steeply.

I hope I don't fall, I thought, a heavy knot of fear tightening my stomach. I pictured myself falling and falling down an endless, dark hole.

Mainly, I didn't want to fall in front of Sari. I knew she'd never let me forget it.

Uncle Ben handed Sari and me bright yellow hard hats. They had lights built into them, like miners' hats. "Stick close together," he instructed. "I remember last summer. You two wandered off and got us into a lot of trouble."

"W-we won't," I stammered. I was trying not to sound nervous, but I couldn't help it.

I glanced at Sari. She was adjusting the yellow hard hat over her hair. She seemed as calm and confident as ever.

"I'll lead the way," Uncle Ben said, tightening his chin strap. He turned and started to lower himself into the hole.

But a shrill cry from behind us made us all stop and turn around.

"Stop! Please—stop! Don't go in!"

A young woman came running across the sand. Her long black hair flew behind her head as she ran. She carried a brown briefcase in one hand. A camera, strapped around her neck, bobbed in front of her.

She stopped in front of us and smiled at Uncle Ben. "Dr. Hassad?" she asked breathlessly.

My uncle nodded. "Yes?" He waited for her to catch her breath.

Wow. She's really pretty, I thought. Her long black hair was sleek and shiny. She had bangs cut straight across her forehead. Beneath the bangs were the most beautiful green eyes I'd ever seen.

She was dressed all in white. A white suit jacket and a white blouse over white slacks. She was short—only an inch or two taller than Sari.

She must be a movie star or something, I told myself. *She's so great looking!*

She set her briefcase down on the sand and brushed back her long black hair. "I'm sorry I shouted like that, Dr. Hassad," she told my uncle. "It's just that I needed to talk to you. I didn't want you to disappear into the pyramid."

Uncle Ben narrowed his eyes at her, studying her. "How did you get past the security guard?" he asked, pulling off the hard hat.

"I showed them my press card," she replied. "I'm a reporter for the Cairo *Sun*. My name is Nila Rahmad. I was hoping—"

"Nila?" Uncle Ben interrupted. "What a pretty name."

She smiled. "Yes. My mother named me after the River of Life, the Nile."

"Well, it's a very pretty name," Uncle Ben replied. His eyes twinkled. "But I'm not ready to have any reporters write about our work here."

Nila frowned and bit her lower lip. "I spoke to Dr. Fielding a few days ago," she said.

My uncle's eyes widened in surprise. "You did?"

"Dr. Fielding gave me permission to write about your discovery," Nila insisted, her green eyes locked on my uncle.

"Well, we haven't discovered anything yet!" Uncle Ben said sharply. "There may not be anything to discover."

"That's not what Dr. Fielding told me," Nila replied. "He seemed confident that you were about to make a discovery that would shock the world."

Uncle Ben laughed. "Sometimes my partner gets excited and talks too much," he told Nila.

Nila's eyes pleaded with my uncle. "May I come into the pyramid with you?" She glanced at Sari and me. "I see you have other visitors."

"My daughter, Sari, and my nephew, Gabe," Uncle Ben replied.

"Well, could I come down with them?" Nila pleaded. "I promise I won't write a word for my paper until you give me permission."

Uncle Ben rubbed his chin thoughtfully. He swung the hard hat back onto his head. "No photographs, either," he muttered.

"Does that mean I can come?" Nila asked excitedly.

Uncle Ben nodded. "As an observer." He was trying to act real tough. But I could see he liked her.

Nila flashed him a warm smile. "Thank you, Dr. Hassad."

He reached into the storage cart and handed her a yellow hard hat. "We won't be making any amazing discoveries today," he warned her. "But we're getting very close—to something."

As she slipped on the heavy helmet, Nila turned to Sari and me. "Is this your first time in the pyramid?" she asked.

"No way. I've already been down three times," Sari boasted. "It's really awesome."

"I just arrived yesterday," I said. "So it's my first time down in—"

I stopped when I saw Nila's expression change.

Why was she staring at me like that?

I glanced down and realized that she was staring at the amber pendant. Her mouth was open in shock.

"No! I don't believe this! I really don't! This is so *weird*!" she exclaimed.

"Wh-what's wrong?" I stammered.

"We're *twins*!" Nila declared. She reached under her suit jacket and pulled out a pendant she wore around her neck.

An amber pendant, shaped exactly like mine.

"How unusual!" Uncle Ben exclaimed.

Nila grasped my pendant between her fingers and lowered her face to examine it. "You have a scarab inside yours," she told me, turning the pendant around in her fingers.

She dropped mine and held hers up for me to see. "Look, Gabe. Mine is empty."

I gazed into her pendant. It looked like clear orange glass. Nothing inside.

"I think *yours* is prettier," Sari told Nila. "I wouldn't want to wear a dead bug around my neck."

"But it's supposed to be good luck or something," Nila replied. She tucked the pendant back under her white jacket. "I hope it isn't *bad* luck to have an empty one!"

"I hope so, too," Uncle Ben commented dryly. He turned and led us into the pyramid opening.

I'm not really sure how I got lost.

Sari and I were walking together behind Uncle Ben and Nila. We were close behind them. I could hear my uncle explaining about how the tunnel walls were granite and limestone.

Our helmet lights were on. The narrow beams of yellow light darted and crisscrossed over the dusty tunnel floor and walls as we made our way deeper and deeper into the pyramid.

The ceiling hung low, and we all had to stoop as we walked. The tunnel kept curving, and there were several smaller tunnels that branched off. "False starts and dead ends," Uncle Ben called them.

It was hard to see in the flickering light from our helmets. I stumbled once and scraped my elbow against the rough tunnel wall. It was surprisingly cool down here, and I wished I had worn a sweatshirt.

Up ahead, Uncle Ben was telling Nila about King Tut and Prince Khor-Ru. It sounded to me as if Uncle Ben was trying to impress her. I wondered if he had a crush on her or something.

"This is so thrilling!" I heard Nila exclaim. "It was so nice of Dr. Fielding and you to let me see it."

"Who is Dr. Fielding?" I whispered to Sari.

"My father's partner," Sari whispered back. "But Daddy doesn't like him. You'll probably meet him. He's always around. I don't like him much, either."

I stopped to examine a strange-looking marking on the tunnel wall. It was shaped like some kind of animal head. "Sari—look!" I whispered. "An ancient drawing."

Sari rolled her eyes. "It's Bart Simpson," she muttered. "One of Daddy's workers must have drawn it there."

"I knew that!" I lied. "I was just testing you."

When was I going to stop making a fool of myself in front of my cousin?

I turned back from the stupid drawing on the wall—and Sari had vanished.

I could see the narrow beam of light from her hard hat up ahead. "Hey—wait up!" I called. But the light disappeared as the tunnel curved away.

And then I stumbled again.

My helmet hit the tunnel wall. And the light went out.

"Hey—Sari? Uncle Ben?" I called to them. I leaned heavily against the wall, afraid to move in the total darkness.

"Hey! Can anybody hear me?" My voice echoed down the narrow tunnel.

But no one replied.

I pulled off the hard hat and fiddled with the light. I turned it, trying to tighten it. Then I shook the whole hat. But the light wouldn't come back on.

Sighing, I strapped the hat back onto my head.

Now what? I thought, starting to feel a little afraid. My stomach began fluttering. My throat suddenly felt dry.

"Hey — can anybody hear me?" I shouted. "I'm in the dark back here. I can't walk!"

No reply.

Where *were* they? Didn't they notice that I had disappeared?

"Well, I'll just wait right here for them," I murmured to myself.

I leaned my shoulder against the tunnel wall — — and fell right through.

No way to catch my balance. Nothing to grab on to.

I was falling, falling down through total darkness.

My hands flailed wildly as I fell.

I reached out frantically for something to grab on to.

It all happened too fast to cry out.

I landed hard on my back. Pain shot out through my arms and legs. The darkness swirled around me.

My breath was knocked right out of me. I saw bright flashes of red, then everything went black again. I struggled to breathe but couldn't suck in any air.

I had that horrible heavy feeling in my chest, like when a basketball hits you in the stomach.

Finally, I sat up, struggling to see in the total darkness. I heard a soft, shuffling sound. Something scraping over the hard dirt floor.

"Hey—can anyone hear me?" My voice came out a hoarse whisper.

Now my back ached, but I was starting to breathe normally.

"Hey — I'm down here!" I called, a little louder.

No reply.

Didn't they miss me? Weren't they looking for me?

I was leaning back on my hands, starting to feel better. My right hand started to itch.

I reached to scratch it and brushed something away.

And realized my legs were itching, too. And felt something crawling on my left wrist.

I shook my hand hard. "What's going on here?" I whispered to myself.

My entire body tingled. I felt soft pinpricks up my arms and legs.

Shaking both arms, I jumped to my feet. And banged my helmet against a low ledge.

The light flickered on.

I gasped when I saw the crawling creatures in the narrow beam of light.

Spiders. Hundreds of bulby white spiders, thick on the chamber floor.

They scuttled across the floor, climbing over each other. As I jerked my head up and the light swept up with it, I saw that the stone walls were covered with them, too. The white spiders made the wall appear to move as if it were alive.

Spiders hung on invisible threads from the chamber ceiling. They seemed to bob and float in midair.

I shook one off the back of my hand.

And with a gasp, realized why my legs itched. Spiders were crawling all over them. Up over my arms. Down my back.

"Help—somebody! Please!" I managed to cry out.

I felt a spider drop onto the back of my neck.

I brushed it away with a frantic slap. "Somebody—help me!" I screamed. "Can anyone hear me?"

And then I saw something scarier. Much scarier. A snake slid down from above me, lowering itself rapidly toward my face.

I ducked and tried to cover my face as the snake silently dropped toward me.

"Grab it!" I heard someone call. "Grab on to it!"

With a startled cry, I raised my eyes. The light beam followed. And I saw that it was not a snake that stretched from above — but a rope.

"Grab on to it, Gabe! Hurry!" Sari shouted urgently from high above.

Brushing away spiders, kicking frantically to shake the spiders off my sneakers, I grasped the rope with both hands.

And felt myself being tugged up, pulled up through the darkness to the tunnel floor above.

A few seconds later, Uncle Ben reached down and grabbed me under the arms. As he hoisted me up, I could see Sari and Nila pulling with all their might on the rope.

I cheered happily as my feet touched solid ground. But I didn't have long to celebrate. My entire body felt as if it were on fire!

I went wild, kicking my legs, brushing spiders off my arms, scratching spiders off my back, stamping on the spiders as they scuttled off me.

Glancing up, I saw that Sari was laughing at me. "Gabe, what do you call that dance?" she asked.

Uncle Ben and Nila laughed, too. "How did you fall down there, Gabe?" my uncle demanded, peering down into the spider chamber.

"The wall—it gave way," I told him, frantically scratching my legs.

"I thought you were still with me," Sari explained. "When I turned around . . . " Her voice trailed off.

The light on Uncle Ben's helmet beamed down to the lower chamber. "That's a long fall," Uncle Ben said, turning back to me. "Are you sure you're okay?"

I nodded. "Yeah. I guess. It knocked the wind out of me. And then the spiders—"

"There must be hundreds of chambers like that," my uncle commented, glancing at Nila. "The pyramid builders made a maze of tunnels and chambers—to fool tomb robbers and keep them from finding the real tomb."

"Yuck! Such fat spiders!" Sari groaned, stepping back.

43

"There are millions of them down there," I told her. "On the walls, hanging from the ceiling—everywhere."

"This is going to give me bad dreams," Nila said softly, moving closer to Uncle Ben.

"You sure you're okay?" my uncle demanded again.

I started to reply. Then I suddenly remembered something. The mummy hand. It was tucked in my back pocket.

Had it been crushed when I landed on it?

My heart skipped a beat. I didn't want anything bad to happen to that little hand. It was my good luck charm.

I reached into my jeans pocket and pulled it out. Holding it under the light from my hard hat, I examined it carefully.

I breathed a sigh of relief when I saw that it was okay. It still felt cold. But it hadn't been crushed.

"What's that?" Nila asked, leaning closer to see it better. She brushed her long hair away from her face. "Is that the Summoner?"

"How did you know that?" I demanded, holding the hand up so she could see it better.

Nila stared at it intently. "I know a lot about ancient Egypt," she replied. "I've studied it my whole life."

"It might be an ancient relic," Uncle Ben broke in.

44

"Or it might just be a tacky souvenir," Sari added.

"It has real powers," I insisted, brushing it off carefully. "I landed on it down there"—I pointed to the spider chamber—"and it didn't get crushed."

"I guess it *is* a good luck charm," Nila said, turning back to Uncle Ben.

"Then why didn't it keep Gabe from falling through that wall?" Sari cracked.

Before I could answer, I saw the mummy hand move. The tiny fingers slowly curled. Out and then in.

I cried out and nearly dropped it.

"Gabe—now what?" Uncle Ben demanded sharply.

"Uh . . . nothing," I replied.

They wouldn't believe me anyway.

"I think we've done enough exploring for now," Uncle Ben said.

As we made our way to the entrance, I held the mummy hand in front of me.

I wasn't seeing things. I knew that for sure. The fingers really had moved.

But why?

Was the hand trying to signal me? Was it trying to warn me about something?

11

Two days later, Uncle Ben's workers reached the doorway to the burial chamber.

Sari and I had spent the two days hanging around in the tent or exploring the area outside the pyramid. Since it was mostly sand, there wasn't much to explore.

We spent one long afternoon playing game after game of Scrabble. Playing Scrabble with Sari wasn't much fun at all. She was a very defensive player and spent hours figuring out ways to clog the board and block me from getting any good words.

Whenever I put down a really good word, Sari claimed it wasn't a real word and couldn't be allowed. And since we didn't have a dictionary in the tent, she won most of the arguments.

Uncle Ben, meanwhile, seemed really stressed out. I thought maybe he was nervous about finally opening the tomb.

He barely spoke to Sari and me. Instead, he spent a lot of time meeting with people I didn't recognize. He seemed very serious and businesslike. None of his usual backslapping and joking.

Uncle Ben also spent a lot of time talking with Nila. At first, she'd said she wanted to write about his discovery in the pyramid. But now she'd decided to write an article about him. She wrote down nearly every word he said in a little pad she carried with her.

Then, at breakfast, he finally smiled for the first time in two days. "Today's the day," he announced.

Sari and I couldn't hide our excitement. "Are you taking us with you?" I asked.

Uncle Ben nodded. "I want you to be there," he replied. "Perhaps we will make history today. Perhaps it will be a day you will want to remember for the rest of your lives." He shrugged and added thoughtfully: "Perhaps."

A few minutes later, the three of us followed several workers across the sand toward the pyramid. It was a gray day. Heavy clouds hovered low in the sky, threatening rain. The pyramid rose up darkly to meet the clouds.

As we approached the small opening in the back wall, Nila came running up, her camera bobbing in front of her. She wore a long-sleeved blue denim work shirt over loose-fitting faded jeans. Uncle Ben greeted her warmly. "But still no photographs," he told her firmly. "Promise?"

Nila smiled back at him. Her green eyes lit up excitedly. She raised a hand to her heart. "Promise."

We all took yellow hard hats from the equipment dump. Uncle Ben was carrying a large stone mallet. He lowered himself into the entrance, and we followed.

My heart was racing as I hurried to keep up with Sari. The lights from our helmets darted over the narrow tunnel. Far up ahead, I could hear the voices of workers and the steady scrape of their digging tools.

"This is really awesome!" I exclaimed breathlessly to Sari.

"Maybe the tomb is filled with jewels," Sari whispered as we made our way around a curve. "Sapphires and rubies and emeralds. Maybe I'll get to try on a jeweled crown worn by an Egyptian princess."

"Do you think there's a mummy in the tomb?" I asked. I wasn't too interested in jewels. "Do you think the mummified body of Prince Khor-Ru is lying there, waiting to be discovered?"

Sari made a disgusted face. "Is that all you can think about — mummies?"

"Well, we *are* in an ancient Egyptian pyramid!" I shot back.

"There could be millions of dollars' worth of jewels and relics in that tomb," Sari scolded. "And all you can think about is some moldy old body wrapped up in tar and gauze." She shook her head. "You know, most kids get over their fascination with mummies by the time they're eight or nine."

"Uncle Ben didn't!" I replied.

That shut her up.

We followed Nila and Uncle Ben in silence. After a while, the narrow tunnel curved up sharply. The air grew warmer as we followed it up.

I could see lights ahead. Two battery-powered spotlights were trained on the far wall. As we drew closer, I realized it wasn't a wall. It was a door.

Four workers—two men and two women— were on their knees, working with small shovels and picks. They were scraping the last chunks of dirt away from the door.

"It looks beautiful!" Uncle Ben cried, running up to the workers. They turned to greet him. "It's awesome in the true sense of the word!" he declared.

Nila, Sari, and I stepped up behind him. Uncle Ben was right. The ancient door really was awesome!

It wasn't very tall. I could see that Uncle Ben would have to stoop to step into it. But it looked like a door fit for a prince.

The dark mahogany wood—now petrified— must have been brought from far away. I knew that kind of wood didn't come from any trees that grew in Egypt.

Strange hieroglyphs covered the door from top to bottom. I recognized birds, and cats, and other animals etched deeply into the dark wood.

The most startling sight of all was the seal that locked the door—a snarling lion's head, sculpted in gold. The light from the spotlights made the lion glow like the sun.

"The gold is soft," I heard one of the workers tell my uncle. "The seal will break away easily."

Uncle Ben lowered his heavy mallet to the ground. He stared for a long moment at the glowing lion's head, then turned back to us. "They thought this lion would scare any intruders away from the tomb," he explained. "I guess it worked. Till now."

"Dr. Hassad, I have to photograph the actual breaking of the seal," Nila said, stepping up beside him. "You really must let me. We can't let the moment go unrecorded."

He gazed at her thoughtfully. "Well . . . okay," he agreed.

A pleased smile crossed her face as she raised her camera. "Thanks, Ben."

The workers stepped back. One of them handed Uncle Ben a hammer and a delicate tool that looked like a doctor's scalpel. "It's all yours, Dr. Hassad," she said.

Uncle Ben raised the tools and stepped up to the seal. "Once I break this seal, we will open the door and step into a room that hasn't been seen in three thousand years," he announced.

Nila steadied her camera over her eyes, carefully adjusting the lens.

Sari and I moved up beside the workers.

The gold lion appeared to glow brighter as Uncle Ben raised the tool. A hush fell over the tunnel. I could feel the excitement, feel the tension in the air.

Such suspense!

I realized I had been holding my breath. I let it out in a long, silent whoosh and took another.

I glanced at Sari. She was nervously chewing her lower lip. Her hands were pressed tightly at her sides.

"Anyone hungry? Maybe we should forget about this and send out for a pizza!" Uncle Ben joked.

We all laughed loudly.

That was Uncle Ben for you—cracking a dumb joke at what might be the most exciting moment of his life.

The tense silence returned. Uncle Ben's expression turned serious. He turned back to the ancient seal. He raised the small chisel to the back of the seal. Then he started to lift the hammer.

And a booming voice rang out, "PLEASE—LET ME REST IN PEACE!"

I let out a startled cry.

"LET ME REST IN PEACE!" the booming voice repeated.

I saw Uncle Ben lower his chisel. He spun around, his eyes wide with surprise.

I realized the voice came from behind us. I turned to see a man I had never seen before, half hidden in the shadowy tunnel. He made his way toward us, taking long, steady strides.

He was a tall, lanky man, so tall he really had to hunch his shoulders in the low tunnel. Bald except for a fringe of dark hair at the ears, he had a slender face, an unfriendly scowl on his thin lips.

He wore a perfectly ironed safari jacket over a shirt and necktie. His black eyes, like little raisins, glared at my uncle. I wondered if the man ever ate. He was as skinny as a mummy himself!

"Omar!" Uncle Ben started. "I wasn't expecting you back from Cairo."

"Let me rest in peace," Dr. Fielding repeated, softer this time. "Those are the words of Prince Khor-Ru. Written on the ancient stone we found last month. That was the prince's wish."

"Omar, we've been over this before," my uncle replied, sighing. He lowered the hammer and chisel to his sides.

Dr. Fielding pushed past Sari and me as if we weren't there. He stopped in front of my uncle and swept a hand back over his bald head. "Well, then, how can you dare to break the seal?" Dr. Fielding demanded.

"I am a scientist," my uncle replied slowly, speaking each word clearly and distinctly. "I cannot allow superstition to stand in the way of discovery, Omar."

"I am also a scientist," Dr. Fielding replied, using both hands to tighten his necktie. "But I am not willing to defile this ancient tomb. I am not willing to go against the wishes of Prince Khor-Ru. And I am not willing to call the words of the hieroglyph mere superstition."

"This is where we disagree," Uncle Ben said softly. He motioned to the four workers. "We have spent too many months, too many years, to stop just outside the door. We have come this far, Omar. We must go the rest of the way."

Dr. Fielding chewed his lower lip. He pointed to the top of the door. "Look, Ben. There are the same hieroglyphs as on the stone. The same warning. *Let me rest in peace.*"

"I know, I know," my uncle said, frowning.

"The warning is very clear," Dr. Fielding continued heatedly, his tiny raisin eyes narrowed at my uncle. "If anyone should disturb the prince, if anyone should repeat the ancient words written on the tomb five times—the mummified prince shall come to life. And he shall seek his vengeance on those who disturbed him."

Listening to those words made me shudder. I stared hard at Uncle Ben. Why hadn't he ever told Sari and me about the prince's threat? Why hadn't he ever mentioned the words of warning they had found on an ancient stone?

Was he afraid he might frighten us?

Was he frightened himself?

No. No way.

He didn't seem at all frightened now as he argued with Dr. Fielding. I could tell they had had this argument before. And I could see there was no way that Dr. Fielding was going to stop my uncle from breaking the seal and entering the tomb.

"This is my final warning, Ben—" Dr. Fielding said. "For the sake of everyone here . . ." He motioned with one hand to the four workers.

"Superstition," Uncle Ben replied. "I cannot be stopped by superstition. I am a scientist." He raised the chisel and hammer. "The seal will be broken."

Dr. Fielding tossed up both hands in disgust. "I will not be a party to this," he declared. He spun around, nearly hitting his head on the tunnel ceiling. Then, muttering to himself, he hurried away, disappearing quickly into the darkness of the tunnel.

Uncle Ben took a couple of steps after him. "Omar? Omar?"

But we could hear Dr. Fielding's footsteps growing fainter as he made his way out of the pyramid.

Uncle Ben sighed and leaned close to me. "I don't trust that man," he muttered. "He doesn't really care about the old superstitions. He wants to steal this discovery for himself. That's why he tried to make me stop outside the door."

I didn't know how to reply. My uncle's words startled me. I thought scientists had rules about who took credit for what discoveries.

Uncle Ben whispered something to Nila. Then he made his way back to the four workers. "If any of you agree with Dr. Fielding," he told them, "you are free to leave now."

The workers exchanged glances with one another.

"You have all heard the words of warning on the tomb door. I do not want to force anyone to enter the tomb," Uncle Ben told them.

"But we have worked so hard," one of the men said. "We cannot stop here. We have no choice. We *have* to open that door."

A smile crossed my uncle's face. "I agree," he said, turning back to the lion seal.

I glanced at Sari and realized that she was already staring at me. "Gabe, if you're scared, Daddy will let you leave," she whispered. "You don't have to be embarrassed."

She never quits!

"I'm staying," I whispered back. "But if you want me to walk you back to the tent, I will."

A loud *clink* made us both turn back to the door. Uncle Ben was working to pry off the gold lion seal. Nila had her camera poised. The workers stood tensely, watching Uncle Ben's every move.

Uncle Ben worked slowly, carefully. He slid the chisel behind the ancient seal and gently pried and scraped.

A few minutes later, the seal fell into my uncle's hands. Nila busily snapped photograph after photograph. Uncle Ben carefully passed it to one of the workers. "That's not a Christmas gift," he joked. "I'm keeping that for my mantelpiece!"

Everyone laughed.

Uncle Ben gripped the edge of the door with both hands. "I'm going in first," he announced. "If I'm not back in twenty minutes, go tell Dr. Fielding he was right!"

More laughter.

Two of the workers moved to help Uncle Ben slide open the door. They pressed their shoulders against it, straining hard.

The door didn't budge.

"It might need a little oiling," Uncle Ben joked. "After all, it's been closed for three thousand years."

They worked for several minutes with picks and chisels, carefully freeing the door. Then they tried once again, pressing their shoulders against the heavy mahogany door.

"Yes!" Uncle Ben cried out as the door slid an inch.

Then another inch. Another inch.

Everyone pressed forward, eager to get a view of the ancient tomb.

Two of the workers moved the large spotlights, aiming them into the doorway.

As Uncle Ben and his two helpers pushed against the door, Sari and I stepped up beside Nila. "Isn't this amazing!" Nila cried excitedly. "I can't believe I'm the only reporter here! I'm so lucky!"

I'm lucky, too, I realized. *How many kids would give anything to be standing right where*

58

I am? How many kids would love to be one of the first people in the world to step into a three-thousand-year-old tomb in an Egyptian pyramid?

The faces of some of my friends back home suddenly popped into my mind. I realized I couldn't *wait* to tell them about my adventure here!

The door scraped noisily against the dirt floor. Another inch. Another inch.

The opening was almost big enough for a person to squeeze through.

"Move the light a little," Uncle Ben instructed. "Another few inches, and we can go in and shake hands with the prince."

The door scraped open another inch. With a great heave, Uncle Ben and his helpers forced it open another few inches.

"Yes!" he cried happily.

Nila snapped a photograph.

We all pressed forward eagerly.

Uncle Ben slid through the opening first.

Sari bumped me out of the way and cut in front of me.

My heart was pounding hard. My hands were suddenly ice-cold.

I didn't care who went in first. I just wanted to go in!

One by one, we slipped into the ancient chamber.

Finally, my turn came. I took a deep breath, slipped through the opening, and saw—

—nothing.

Except for a lot of cobwebs, the chamber was bare.

Totally bare.

I let out a long sigh. Poor Uncle Ben. All that work for nothing. I felt so disappointed.

I glanced around the bare chamber. The spotlights made the thick cobwebs glow like silver. Our shadows stretched across the dirt floor like ghosts.

I turned to Uncle Ben, expecting him to be disappointed, too. But to my surprise, he had a smile on his face. "Move the lights," he told one of the workers. "And bring the tools. We have another seal to remove."

He pointed across the empty room to the back wall. In the gray light, I could make out the outline of a door. Another sculpted lion sealed it shut.

"I *knew* this wasn't the real burial chamber!" Sari cried, grinning at me.

"As I said, the Egyptians often did this," Uncle Ben explained. "They built several false chambers to hide the real chamber from grave robbers." He pulled off his hard hat and scratched his hair. "In fact," he continued, "we may find several empty chambers before we find Prince Khor-Ru's resting place."

Nila snapped a photo of Uncle Ben examining the newly discovered door. She smiled at me. "You should have seen the expression on your face, Gabe," she said. "You looked so disappointed."

"I thought—" I started. But the scrape of Uncle Ben's chisel against the seal made me stop.

We all turned to watch him work at the seal. Staring across the cobweb-filled chamber, I tried to imagine what waited for us on the other side of the door.

Another empty chamber? Or a three-thousand-year-old Egyptian prince, surrounded by all of his treasures and belongings?

Work on the door went slowly. We all broke for lunch and then returned. That afternoon Uncle Ben and his helpers worked for another couple of hours, carefully trying to remove the seal without damaging it.

As they worked, Sari and I sat on the floor and watched. The air was hot and kind of sour. I guess it was ancient air. Sari and I talked about last year and the adventures we'd had in the Great Pyramid. Nila snapped our picture.

"Almost got it," Uncle Ben announced.

We all started to get excited again. Sari and I climbed to our feet and crossed the room to get a better view.

The lion seal slid free from the door. Two of the workers placed it gently into a padded crate. Then Uncle Ben and the other two workers set to work pushing open the door.

This door proved even more difficult than the last. "It's . . . really . . . stuck," Uncle Ben groaned. He and the workers pulled out more tools and began prying and chipping away the hard crust that had formed on the doorway over the centuries.

An hour later, they got the door to slide an inch. Then another inch. Another.

When it had slid halfway open, Uncle Ben removed the light from his helmet and beamed it through the opening. He peered into the next chamber for the longest time without saying a word.

Sari and I moved closer. My heart began racing again.

What did he see? I wondered. What was he staring at so silently?

Finally, Uncle Ben lowered the light and turned back to us. "We've made a big mistake," he said quietly.

A shocked silence fell over the room. I swallowed hard, stunned by my uncle's words.

But then a broad smile crossed his face. "We made a mistake by underestimating our discovery!" he exclaimed. "This will be more important than the discovery of King Tut! This tomb is even grander!"

A gleeful cheer echoed against the stone walls. The workers rushed forward to shake Uncle Ben's hand and offer their congratulations.

"Congratulations to us all!" Uncle Ben declared happily.

We were all laughing and talking excitedly as we slipped through the narrow opening, into the next chamber.

As the lights beamed over the vast room, I knew I was seeing something I would never forget. Even the thick layer of dust and cobwebs could not cover the amazing treasures that filled the chamber.

My eyes darted quickly around. I struggled to focus on it all. But there was too much to see! I actually felt dizzy.

The walls were covered from floor to ceiling with hieroglyphs, etched into the stone. The floor was cluttered with furniture and other objects. It looked more like someone's attic or a storeroom than a tomb!

A tall, straight-backed throne caught my eye. It had a golden radiating sun etched into the seat back. Behind it, I saw chairs and benches and a long couch.

Against the wall were stacked dozens of stone and clay jars. Some were cracked and broken. But many were in perfect condition.

A gold monkey head lay on its side in the middle of the floor. Behind it, I saw several large chests.

Uncle Ben and one of the workers carefully pulled back the lid of one of the chests. Their eyes grew wide as they gaped inside.

"Jewelry!" Uncle Ben declared. "It's filled with gold jewelry!"

Sari came up beside me, an excited grin on her face.

"This is *awesome*!" I whispered.

She nodded agreement. "Awesome!"

We whispered in the heavy silence. No one else talked. Everyone was too overwhelmed by the amazing sight. The loudest sound was the clicking of Nila's camera.

Uncle Ben stepped between Sari and me and placed a hand on our shoulders. "Isn't this unbelievable?" he cried. "It's all in perfect condition. Untouched for three thousand years."

When I glanced up at him, I saw that he had tears in his eyes. *This is the greatest moment of Uncle Ben's life*, I realized.

"We must be very careful—" Uncle Ben started. But he stopped in midsentence, and I saw his expression change.

As he guided Sari and me across the room, I saw what he was staring at. A large stone mummy case, hidden in shadow, stood against the far wall.

"Oh, wow!" I murmured as we stepped up to it.

Made of smooth gray stone, the heavy lid had a long crack down the center.

"Is the prince buried inside it?" Sari asked eagerly.

It took Uncle Ben a moment to reply. He stood between us, his eyes locked on the ancient mummy case. "We'll soon see," he finally replied.

As he and the four workers struggled to move the lid, Nila lowered her camera and stepped forward to watch. Her green eyes stared intensely as the lid slowly slid away.

Inside was a coffin the shape of the mummy. It wasn't very long. And it was narrower than I thought it would be.

The workers slowly pried open the coffin's lid. I gasped and grabbed Uncle Ben's hand as the mummy was revealed.

It looked so tiny and frail!

"Prince Khor-Ru," Uncle Ben muttered, staring down into the stone case.

The prince lay on his back, his slender arms crossed over his chest. Black tar had seeped through the bandages. The gauze had worn away from the head, revealing the tar-covered skull.

As I leaned over the case, my heart in my throat, the tar-blackened eyes seemed to stare helplessly up at me.

There's a real person inside there, I thought, feeling a chill run down my spine. *He's about my size. And he died. And they covered him with hot tar and cloth. And he's been lying in this case for three thousand years.*

A real person. A royal prince.

I stared at the cracked tar that covered his face. At the gauzelike cloth, all frayed and yellowed. At the stiff body, so frail and small.

He was alive once, I thought. *Did he ever dream that three thousand years later, people would open his coffin and stare at him? Stare at his mummified body?*

I took a step back to catch my breath. It was *too* exciting.

I saw that Nila also had tears in her eyes. She rested both hands on the edge of the case and leaned over the prince's body, her eyes locked on the blackened face.

"These may be the best-preserved remains ever found," Uncle Ben said quietly. "Of course, we will have to do many tests to determine the young man's identity. But, judging from everything else in this chamber, I think it's safe to say . . ."

His voice trailed off as we all heard sounds from the outer chamber. Footsteps. Voices.

I spun around toward the doorway as four black-uniformed police officers burst into the room. "Okay. Everybody take one step back," one of them ordered, lowering his hand to the gun holster at his side.

Startled cries filled the room. Uncle Ben spun around, his eyes wide with surprise. "What is happening?" he cried.

The four Cairo police officers, their features set in hard frowns, moved quickly into the center of the room.

"Be careful!" Uncle Ben warned, standing in front of the mummy case as if protecting it. "Do not move anything. It is all terribly fragile."

He pulled off the hard hat. His eyes went from officer to officer. "What are you doing here?"

"I asked them to come," a voice boomed from the doorway.

Dr. Fielding entered, a pleased expression on his face. His tiny eyes danced excitedly.

"Omar — I don't understand," Uncle Ben said, taking a few steps toward the other scientist.

"I thought it best to protect the contents of the tomb," Dr. Fielding replied. He gazed quickly around the room, taking in the treasures.

"Wonderful! This is wonderful!" he cried. He stepped forward and shook my uncle's hand enthusiastically. "Congratulations, every- one!" he boomed. "This is almost too much to believe."

Uncle Ben's expression softened. "I still do not understand the need for them," he said, motioning to the grim-faced officers. "No one in this room is about to steal anything."

"Certainly not," Dr. Fielding replied, still squeezing Uncle Ben's hand. "Certainly not. But word will soon get out, Ben. And I thought we should be prepared to guard what we have found."

Uncle Ben eyed the four officers suspi- ciously. But then he shrugged his broad shoulders. "Perhaps you are right," he told Dr. Fielding. "Perhaps you are being smart."

"Just ignore them," Dr. Fielding replied. He slapped my uncle on the back. "I owe you an apol- ogy, Ben. I was wrong to try to stop you before. As a scientist, I should have known better. We owed it to the world to open this tomb. I hope you'll forgive me. We have much to celebrate — don't we!"

* * *

"I don't trust him," Uncle Ben confided that evening as we walked from the tent to dinner. "I don't trust my partner at all."

It was a clear night, surprisingly cool. The purple sky was dotted with a million twinkling white stars. A steady breeze made the palm trees sway on the horizon. The big campfire up ahead dipped and shifted with the wind.

"Is Dr. Fielding coming with us to dinner?" Sari asked. She wore a pale green sweater pulled down over black leggings.

Uncle Ben shook his head. "No, he hurried to phone Cairo. I think he's eager to tell our backers the good news."

"He seemed really excited when he saw the mummy and everything," I said, glancing at the pyramid rising darkly to the evening sky.

"Yes, he did," my uncle admitted. "He certainly changed his mind in a hurry! But I'm keeping my eye on him. Omar would like nothing better than to take over the project. I'm going to keep an eye on those police officers of his, too."

"Daddy, this should be a happy night," Sari scolded. "Let's not talk about Dr. Fielding. Let's just talk about Prince Khor-Ru and how you're going to be rich and famous!"

Uncle Ben laughed. "It's a deal," he told her.

Nila waited for us by the campfire. Uncle Ben had invited her to join us for a barbecue. She wore a white sweatshirt over loose-fitting jeans. Her

71

amber pendant caught the light from the half-moon just rising over the tents.

She looked really pretty. She flashed Uncle Ben a warm smile as we came near. I could tell by his face that he liked her.

"Sari, you're taller than Gabe, aren't you!" Nila commented.

Sari grinned. She loved being taller than me, even though I'm a little older.

"Less than an inch," I said quickly.

"People are definitely getting taller," Nila said to my uncle. "Prince Khor-Ru was so short. He'd be a midget today!"

"It makes you wonder why such short people built such tall pyramids," Uncle Ben said, grinning.

Nila smiled and took his arm.

Sari and I exchanged glances. I could see what Sari was thinking. Her expression said: What's up with those two?

We had a great dinner. Uncle Ben burned the hamburger rolls a little. But no one really minded.

Sari downed two hamburgers. I could only eat one. That gave her something else to boast about.

I was really getting fed up with my bragging cousin. I found myself trying to think of a way to get back at her.

Nila and Uncle Ben kidded around a lot.

"That burial chamber looked like a movie set," Nila teased my uncle. "It was all too perfect. All that gold. And that perfect little mummy. It's all a fake. That's what I'm going to write in my article."

Uncle Ben laughed. He turned to me. "Did you check out the mummy, Gabe? Was this one wearing a wristwatch?"

I shook my head. "No wristwatch."

"See?" Uncle Ben told Nila. "No wristwatch. So it's *got* to be real!"

"I guess that proves it," Nila said, smiling warmly at my uncle.

"Daddy, do you know the words to bring the mummy to life?" Sari broke in. "You know. The words on the tomb that Dr. Fielding was talking about?"

Uncle Ben swallowed the last bite of his hamburger. He wiped the grease off his chin with a napkin. "I can't believe that a serious scientist would believe such superstition," he murmured.

"But what *are* the six words to bring the mummy to life?" Nila demanded. "Come on, Ben. Tell us."

Uncle Ben's smile faded. He shook his finger at Nila. "Oh, no!" he declared. "I don't trust you. If I tell you the words, you'll bring the mummy back to life just to get a good photograph for your newspaper!"

We all laughed.

We were sitting around the campfire, its orange light flickering over our faces. Uncle Ben set his plate down on the ground and spread his hands over the fire.

"*Teki Kahru Teki Kahra Teki Khari!*" he chanted in a deep voice, waving his hands over the flames.

The fire crackled. A twig made a loud popping sound that made my heart skip a beat.

"Are those the secret words?" Sari demanded.

Uncle Ben nodded solemnly. "Those are the words of the hieroglyphs over the entrance to the tomb."

"So maybe the mummy just sat up and stretched?" Sari asked.

"I'd be very surprised," Uncle Ben replied, climbing to his feet. "You're forgetting, Sari—you have to chant the words five times."

"Oh." Sari stared thoughtfully into the fire.

I repeated the words in my mind. *"Teki Kahru Teki Kahra Teki Khari!"* I needed to memorize the words. I had a plan to scare Sari.

"Where are you going?" Nila asked my uncle.

"To the communications tent," he replied. "I have to make a phone call." He turned and made his way quickly over the sand toward the row of canvas tents.

Nila let out a surprised laugh. "He didn't even say good night."

"Daddy's always like that," Sari explained, "when he has something on his mind."

"Guess I'd better go, too," Nila said, climbing to her feet and brushing sand off her jeans. "I'm going to start writing my story for the paper."

She said good night and walked quickly away, her sandals making a slapping sound against the sand.

Sari and I sat staring into the crackling fire. The half-moon had floated high in the sky. Its pale light reflected off the top of the pyramid in the distance.

"Nila is right," I told Sari. "It really did look like a movie set in there."

Sari didn't reply. She stared into the fire without blinking, thinking hard. Something in the fire popped again. The sound seemed to snap her out of her thoughts.

"Do you think Nila likes Daddy?" she asked me, her dark eyes locking on mine.

"Yeah, I guess," I replied. "She's always giving him this smile." I imitated Nila's smile. "And she's always kind of teasing him."

Sari thought about my reply. "And do you think Daddy likes her?"

I grinned. "For sure." I stood up. I was eager to get back to the tent. I wanted to scare Sari.

We walked toward the tents in silence. I guessed that Sari was still thinking about her dad and Nila.

The night air was cool, but it was warm inside the tent. Moonlight filtered through the canvas. Sari pulled her trunk out from under her cot and got down on her knees to search through her clothes.

"Sari," I whispered. "Dare me to recite the ancient words five times?"

"Huh?" She gazed up from the trunk.

"I'm going to chant the words five times," I told her. "You know. See if anything happens."

I expected her to beg me not to. I expected her to get scared and plead: "Please, Gabe—don't do it! Don't! It's too dangerous!"

But instead, Sari turned back to her clothes trunk. "Hey. Give it a try," she told me.

"You sure?" I asked her.

"Yeah. Why not?" she replied, pulling out a pair of denim shorts.

I stared across the tent at her. Was that fear I saw in her eyes? Was she just pretending to be so casual about it?

Yes. I think Sari was a little scared. And trying hard not to show it.

I took a few steps closer and chanted the ancient words in the same low voice Uncle Ben had used: *"Teki Kahru Teki Kahra Teki Khari!"*

Sari dropped the shorts and turned to watch me.

I repeated the chant a second time: *"Teki Kahru Teki Kahra Teki Khari!"*

76

A third time.

A fourth time.

I hesitated. I felt a cold breeze tingle the back of my neck.

Should I chant the words again? Should I go for number five?

I stared down at Sari.

She had closed the trunk lid and was leaning on it tensely, staring back at me. I could see that she was frightened. She chewed her bottom lip.

Should I chant the words for a fifth time?

I felt another chill at the back of my neck.

It's just a superstition, I told myself. *A three-thousand-year-old superstition.*

There's no way that moldy old mummified prince is going to come back to life just because I recite six words I don't even know the meaning of!

No way.

I suddenly thought of all the old movies I had rented about mummies in ancient Egypt. In the movies, the scientists always ignored ancient curses warning them not to disturb the mummies' tombs. Then the mummies always came to life to get their revenge. They staggered around, grabbed the scientists by the throat, and strangled them.

Dumb movies. But I loved them.

Now, staring down at Sari, I saw that she was really scared.

I took a deep breath. I suddenly realized that I felt scared, too.

But it was too late. I had gone too far. I couldn't chicken out now.

"*Teki Kahru Teki Kahra Teki Khari!*" I shouted. The fifth time.

I froze — and waited. I don't know what I expected. A flash of lightning, maybe.

Sari climbed to her feet. She tugged at a strand of dark hair.

"Admit it. You're totally freaked," I said, unable to keep a grin from spreading across my face.

"No way!" she insisted. "Go ahead, Gabe. Chant the words again. Chant them a hundred times! You're not going to scare me! No way!"

But we both gasped when we suddenly saw a dark shadow roll over the tent wall.

And my heart completely stopped when a hoarse voice whispered into the tent: "*Are you in there?*"

My legs trembled as I stumbled back, closer to Sari.

I could see her eyes go wide with surprise — and fear.

The shadow moved quickly toward the tent opening.

We had no time to scream. No time to call for help.

Gaping into the darkness, I saw the flap pull open — and a smooth head poked into the tent.

"Ohhh." I let out a terrified moan as the dark figure slumped toward us.

The mummy is alive! The horrifying thought swept through my mind as I backed away. *The mummy is alive!*

"Dr. Fielding!" Sari cried.

"Huh?" I squinted to see better.

Yes. It was Dr. Fielding.

I struggled to say hello. But my heart was pounding so hard, I couldn't speak. I took a long, deep breath and held it.

"I'm looking for your father," Dr. Fielding told Sari. "I must see him at once. It's extremely urgent."

"He — he's making a phone call," Sari replied in a shaky voice.

Dr. Fielding spun around and ducked out of the tent. The flap snapped shut behind him.

I turned to Sari, my heart still pounding. "He scared me to death!" I confessed. "I thought he was in Cairo. When he poked that skinny, bald head into the tent . . ."

Sari laughed. "He really looks like a mummy — doesn't he?" Her smile faded. "I wonder why he's in such a hurry to see Daddy."

"Let's follow him!" I urged. The idea just popped into my head.

"Yes! Let's go!" I hadn't expected Sari to agree so quickly. But she was already pushing open the tent flap.

I followed her out of the tent. The night had grown cooler. A steady wind made all of the tents appear to shiver.

"Which way did he go?" I whispered.

Sari pointed. "I think that's the communications tent at the end." She started jogging across the sand.

As we ran, the wind blew sand against our legs. I heard music and voices from one of the tents. The workers were celebrating the day's discovery.

The moon cast a strip of light like a carpet along our path. Up ahead, I could see Dr. Fielding's lanky body leaning forward, lurching awkwardly toward the last tent.

He disappeared around the side of it. Sari and I stopped a few tents away. We ducked out of the moonlight, into deep shadows where we wouldn't be seen.

I could hear Dr. Fielding's booming voice from the communications tent. He was talking rapidly, excitedly.

"What is he saying?" Sari whispered.

I couldn't make out the words.

A few seconds later, two figures emerged from the tent. Carrying bright flashlights, they crossed the strip of yellow moonlight, then moved quickly into shadow.

Dr. Fielding appeared to be pulling Uncle Ben, pulling him toward the pyramid.

"What's going on?" Sari whispered, grabbing my sleeve. "Is he *forcing* Daddy to go with him?"

The wind swirled the sand around us. I shivered.

The two men were talking at the same time, shouting and gesturing with their flashlights. *They're arguing about something*, I realized.

Dr. Fielding had a hand on Uncle Ben's shoulder.

Was he shoving Uncle Ben toward the pyramid? Or was Uncle Ben actually leading the way?

It was impossible to tell.

"Let's go," I whispered to Sari.

We stepped away from the tent and started to follow them. We walked slowly, keeping them in view but being careful not to get too close.

"If they turn back, they'll see us," Sari whispered, huddling close to me as we crept over the sand.

She was right. There were no trees or bushes to hide behind here in the open desert.

"Maybe they won't turn back," I replied hopefully.

We crept closer. The pyramid rose up darkly in front of us.

We saw Dr. Fielding and Uncle Ben stop at the opening in the side. I could hear their excited voices, but the wind carried away their words. They still seemed to be arguing.

Uncle Ben disappeared into the pyramid first. Dr. Fielding went in right behind him.

"Did he shove Daddy in?" Sari demanded in a shrill, frightened voice. "It looked like he pushed him inside!"

"I—I don't know," I stammered.

We made our way closer to the entrance. Then we both stopped and stared into the darkness.

I knew we were both thinking the same thing. I knew we both had the same question on our lips:

Should we follow them in?

Sari and I exchanged glances.

The pyramid seemed so much bigger at night, so much darker. The gusting wind howled around its walls as if warning us to stay back.

We crept behind a pile of stones left by the workers. "Let's wait out here for Daddy to come out," Sari suggested.

I didn't argue with her. We had no flashlights, no light of any kind. I didn't think we'd get very far wandering the dark tunnels by ourselves.

I pressed up against the smooth stones and stared at the pyramid opening. Sari gazed up at the half-moon. Thin wisps of cloud floated over it. The ground darkened in front of us.

"You don't think Daddy is in any kind of trouble, do you?" Sari asked. "I mean, he told us he didn't trust Dr. Fielding. And then—"

"I'm sure Uncle Ben is okay," I told her. "I mean, Dr. Fielding is a scientist. He's not a *criminal* or anything."

"But why did he force Daddy into the pyramid in the middle of the night?" Sari asked shrilly. "And what were they arguing about?"

I shrugged in reply. I didn't remember ever seeing Sari so frightened. Normally, I would have enjoyed it. She always bragged about how brave and fearless she was—especially compared to me.

But there was no way I could enjoy this. Mainly because I was just as scared as she was!

It *did* look as if the two scientists were fighting. And it *did* look as if Dr. Fielding pushed Uncle Ben down into the pyramid.

Sari crossed her arms over her sweater and narrowed her eyes at the opening. The wind fluttered her hair, blowing strands across her forehead. But she made no attempt to brush them away.

"What could be so important?" she demanded. "Why did they have to go into the pyramid now? Do you think something was stolen? Aren't those police officers from Cairo down there guarding the place?"

"I saw the four policemen leave," I told her. "They piled into their little car and drove away, just before dinner. I don't know why. Maybe they were called back to the city."

"I—I'm just so confused," Sari admitted. "And worried. I didn't like the look on Dr. Fielding's face. I didn't like the way he was so rude, just bursting into the tent like that. Scaring us to death. Not even saying hi."

"Calm down, Sari," I said softly. "Let's just wait. Everything will be okay."

She let out a sigh but didn't say anything in reply.

We waited in silence. I don't know how much time went by. It seemed like hours and hours.

The slivers of cloud drifted away from the moon. The wind continued to howl eerily around the side of the pyramid.

"Where *are* they? What are they *doing* in there?" Sari demanded.

I started to reply—but stopped when I saw a flicker of light at the pyramid opening.

I grabbed Sari's arm. "Look!" I whispered.

The light grew brighter. A figure emerged, pulling himself out quickly.

Dr. Fielding.

As he stepped into the moonlight, I caught the strange expression on his face. His tiny black eyes were wide and seemed to be rolling around crazily in his head. His eyebrows twitched. His mouth was twisted open. He seemed to be breathing hard.

Dr. Fielding brushed himself off with his hands and began walking away from the pyramid. He was half walking, half staggering, taking long, quick strides with his lanky legs.

"But—where's Daddy?" Sari whispered.

Leaning out from the rocks, I could see the pyramid opening clearly. No light flickered. No sign of Uncle Ben.

"He—he isn't coming out!" Sari stammered.

And before I could react, Sari leaped out from our hiding place behind the stones—and stepped into Dr. Fielding's path.

"Dr. Fielding," she cried loudly, "where is my dad?"

I pushed myself away from the stones and hurried after Sari. I could see Dr. Fielding's eyes spinning wildly. He didn't answer her question.

"Where is my dad?" Sari repeated shrilly.

Dr. Fielding acted as if he didn't see Sari. He stepped past her, walking stiffly, awkwardly, his arms straight down.

"Dr. Fielding?" Sari called after him.

He hurried through the darkness toward the row of tents.

Sari turned back to me, her features tight with fear. "He's done something to Daddy!" she cried. "I *know* he has!"

I turned back to the pyramid opening. Still dark and silent.

The only sound now was the howling of the wind around the stone pyramid wall.

"Dr. Fielding totally ignored me!" Sari cried, her face revealing her anger. "He stormed past me as if I weren't here!"

"I—I know," I stammered weakly.

"And did you see the look on his face?" she demanded. "So evil. So totally evil!"

"Sari—" I started. "Maybe—"

"Gabe, we have to go find Daddy!" Sari interrupted. She grabbed my arm and started pulling me to the pyramid opening. "Hurry!"

"No, Sari, wait!" I insisted, tugging out of her grasp. "We can't go stumbling around the pyramid in the dark. We'll just get lost. We'll never find Uncle Ben!"

"We'll go back to the tent and get lights," she replied. "Quick, Gabe—"

I raised a hand to stop her. "Wait here, Sari," I instructed. "Watch for your dad. Chances are, he'll be climbing out in a few moments. I'll run and get some flashlights."

Staring at the dark opening, she started to argue. But then she changed her mind and agreed to my plan.

My heart pounding, I ran all the way back to the tent. I stopped at the tent opening and gazed down the row of tents, searching for Dr. Fielding.

No sign of him.

In the tent, I grabbed two flashlights. Then I went hurtling back to the pyramid. *Please*, I begged silently as I ran. *Please be out of the pyramid, Uncle Ben. Please be safe.*

But as I frantically made my way over the sand, I could see Sari standing by herself. Even from a distance, I could see her frightened expression as she paced tensely back and forth in front of the pyramid opening.

Uncle Ben, where are you? I wondered. *Why haven't you come out of the pyramid? Are you okay?*

Sari and I didn't say a word. There was no need.

We clicked on the flashlights, then made our way into the pyramid opening. It seemed much steeper than I remembered. I nearly lost my balance, lowering myself to the tunnel floor.

Our lights crisscrossed over the dirt floor. I raised mine to the low ceiling. Keeping the light high, I led the way through the curving tunnel.

Creeping along slowly, I trailed one hand against the wall to steady myself. The wall felt soft and crumbly. Sari kept on my heels, her bright beam of light playing over the floor in front of our feet.

She stopped suddenly as the tunnel curved into a small empty chamber. "How do we know we're going in the right direction?" she asked, her voice a quavering whisper.

I shrugged, breathing hard. "I thought you knew your way," I murmured.

"I've only been down here with Daddy," she replied, her eyes over my shoulders, searching the empty chamber.

"We'll keep going until we find him," I told her, forcing myself to sound braver than I felt.

She stepped in front of me, shining the light over the chamber walls. "Daddy!" she shouted. "Daddy? Can you hear me?"

Her voice echoed down the tunnel. Even the echo sounded frightened.

We froze in place and listened for a reply.
Silence.

"Come on," I urged. I had to lower my head to step into the next narrow tunnel.

Where did it lead? Were we heading toward

90

Prince Khor-Ru's tomb? Is that where we would find Uncle Ben?

Questions, questions. I tried to stop them from coming. But they filled my mind, pestering me, repeating, echoing in my head as we followed the tunnel's curves.

"Daddy? Daddy—where *are* you?" Sari's cries became more frantic as we moved deeper and deeper into the pyramid.

The tunnel curved up steeply, then leveled off. Sari suddenly stopped. Startled, I bumped into her hard, nearly making her drop her flashlight. "Sorry," I whispered.

"Gabe, look!" she cried, pointing her beam of light just ahead of her sneakers. "Footprints!"

I lowered my eyes to the small circle of light. I could see a set of boot prints in the dirt. A heel and spikey bumps. "Work boots," I muttered.

She circled the floor with the light. There were several different prints in the dirt, heading in the same direction we were.

"Does this mean we're going the right way?" she asked.

"Maybe," I replied, studying the prints. "It's hard to tell whether these are new or old."

"Daddy?" Sari shouted eagerly. "Can you hear me?"

No reply.

She frowned and motioned for me to follow. Seeing the many sets of prints gave us new hope, and we moved faster, trailing our hands along the wall to steady ourselves as we made our way.

We both cried out happily when we realized we had reached the outer chamber to the tomb. Our lights played over the ancient hieroglyphs that covered the wall and the doorway.

"Daddy? Daddy?" Sari's voice cut through the heavy silence.

We darted through the empty chamber, then slipped through the opening that led to the tomb. The prince's burial chamber stretched out in front of us, dark and silent.

"Daddy? Daddy?" Sari tried again.

I shouted, too. "Uncle Ben? Are you here?"

Silence.

I swept my light over the room's clutter of treasures, over the heavy chests, the chairs, the stone and clay jars piled in the corner.

"He isn't here," Sari choked out with a disappointed sob.

"Then where did Dr. Fielding bring Uncle Ben?" I asked, thinking out loud. "There's nowhere else in the pyramid that they might come."

Sari's light came to rest on the large stone mummy case. Her eyes narrowed as she studied it.

"Uncle Ben!" I shouted frantically. "Are you in here somewhere?"

Sari grabbed my arm. "Gabe—look!" she cried. Her light remained on the mummy case.

I couldn't figure out what she was trying to show me. "What about it?" I demanded.

"The lid," Sari murmured.

I gazed at the lid. The heavy stone slab covered the case tightly.

"The lid is closed," Sari continued, stepping away from me and toward the mummy case. Her light remained on the lid.

"Yeah. So?" I still didn't understand.

"When we all left this afternoon," Sari explained, "the lid was open. In fact, I remember Daddy telling the workers to leave the lid open for tonight."

"You're right!" I cried.

"Help me, Gabe," Sari pleaded, setting her flashlight down at her feet. "We have to open the mummy case."

I hesitated for a second, feeling a wave of cold fear run down my body. Then I took a deep breath and moved to help Sari.

She was already pushing the stone lid with both hands. I stepped up beside her and pushed, too. Pushed with all my might.

The stone slab slid more easily then I'd guessed.

Working together, Sari and I strained against the lid, pushing . . . pushing.

We moved it about a foot.

Then we both lowered our heads to peer into the mummy's case—and gasped in horror.

"Daddy!" Sari shrieked.

Uncle Ben lay on his back, knees raised, hands at his sides, his eyes shut. Sari and I shoved the heavy stone lid open another foot.

"Is he—? Is he—?" Sari stammered.

I pressed my hand on his chest. His heart was thumping with a steady beat. "He's breathing," I told her.

I leaned into the mummy case. "Uncle Ben? Can you hear me? Uncle Ben?"

He didn't move.

I lifted his hand and squeezed it. It felt warm but limp. "Uncle Ben? Wake up!" I shouted.

His eyes didn't open. I lowered the hand back to the bottom of the mummy case. "He's out cold," I murmured.

Sari stood behind me, both hands pressed against her cheeks. She stared down at Uncle Ben, her eyes wide with fear. "I—I don't believe this!" she cried in a tiny voice. "Dr. Fielding left

Daddy here to smother! If we hadn't come along . . ." Her voice trailed off.

Uncle Ben let out a low groan.

Sari and I stared down at him hopefully. But he didn't open his eyes.

"We have to call the police," I told Sari. "We have to tell them about Dr. Fielding."

"But we can't just leave Daddy here," Sari replied.

I started to reply—but a frightening thought burst into my mind. I felt a shudder of fear roll down my body. "Sari?" I started. "If Uncle Ben is lying in the mummy case . . . then where is the mummy?"

Her mouth dropped open. She stared back at me in stunned silence.

And then we both heard the footsteps.

Slow, scraping footsteps.

And saw the mummy stagger stiffly into the room.

I opened my mouth to scream—but no sound came out.

The mummy lurched stiffly through the chamber doorway. It stared straight ahead with its vacant, tarry eyes. Under the ancient layers of tar, the skull grinned at us.

Scrape. Scrape.

Its feet dragged over the dirt floor, trailing shreds of decaying gauze. Slowly, it raised its arms, making a terrifying cracking sound.

Scrape. Scrape.

My throat tightened in terror. My entire body began to tremble.

I backed away from the mummy case. Sari stood frozen with her hands pressed against her cheeks. I grabbed her arm and pulled her back with me. "Sari—get back! Get back!" I whispered.

She stared in terror at the approaching mummy. I couldn't tell if she heard me or not. I tugged her back farther.

Our backs hit the chamber wall.

The mummy scraped closer. Closer. Staring at us through its vacant, blackened eye sockets, it reached for us with its yellowed, tar-encrusted hands.

Sari let out a shrill shriek.

"Run!" I screamed. "Sari—run!"

But our backs were pressed against the wall. The mummy blocked our path to the doorway.

Moving stiffly, awkwardly, the ancient corpse dragged itself closer.

"This is all my fault!" I declared in a trembling voice. "I said the words five times. I brought it back to life!"

"Wh-what can we do?" Sari cried in a hushed whisper.

I didn't have an answer. "Uncle Ben!" I shrieked desperately. "Uncle Ben—help us!"

But the mummy case remained silent. Even my frantic screams could not awaken my uncle.

Sari and I edged along the chamber wall, our eyes locked on the approaching mummy. Its bandaged feet scraped over the floor, sending up dark clouds of dust as it moved heavily toward us.

A sour smell rose over the room. The smell of a three-thousand-year-old corpse coming to life.

I pressed my back against the cold stone of the chamber wall, my mind racing. The mummy stopped at the mummy case, turned stiffly, and continued lurching toward us.

"Hey!" I cried out as an idea burst into my mind.

My little mummy hand. The Summoner.

Why hadn't I thought of it before? It had saved us last year by raising a group of ancient mummies from the dead.

Could it also summon them to stop? Could it make them die again?

If I raised the little mummy hand up to Prince Khor-Ru, would it stop him long enough for Sari and me to escape?

It was only seconds away from grabbing us.

It was worth a try.

I reached into my back jeans pocket for the mummy hand.

It was gone.

22

"No!" I uttered a surprised cry and frantically grabbed at my other pockets.

No mummy hand.

"Gabe—what's wrong?" Sari demanded.

"The mummy hand—it's gone!" I told her, my voice choked with panic.

Scrape. Scrape.

The foul odor grew stronger as the ancient mummy dragged nearer.

I was desperate to find my mummy hand. But I knew there was no time to think about it now. "We've got to make a run for it," I told Sari. "The mummy is slow and stiff. If we can get past it . . ."

"But what about Daddy?" she cried. "We can't just leave him here."

"We have to," I told her. "We'll get help. We'll come back for him."

The mummy made a brittle cracking sound as

it stepped forward. The sound of an ancient bone breaking.

But it continued toward us, moving stiffly but steadily, its arms outstretched.

"Sari—run—*now!*" I screamed.

I gave her a hard shove to get her going.

The room blurred as I forced myself to move.

The mummy made another loud cracking sound. It leaned its body forward and reached out as we dodged around it.

I tried to duck under the mummy's outstretched hand. But I felt the scrape of its ancient fingers against the back of my neck—cold fingers, hard as a statue.

I knew it was a touch I would never forget.

My neck tingled. I lowered my head from its grasp—and plunged forward.

Sari let out low sobs as she ran. My heart raced as I hurried to catch up to her. I forced myself to run, but my legs felt so heavy, as if they were made of solid stone.

We were nearly to the doorway when we saw a flickering light.

Sari and I both cried out and skidded to a stop as a beam of light swept into the room. Behind the light, a figure stepped into the doorway.

Shielding my eyes from the sudden brightness, I squinted hard, eager to see who it was.

"Nila!" I cried as she raised the flashlight beam to the ceiling. "Nila—help us!" I choked out.

"It's come alive!" Sari shouted to her. "Nila—it's come alive!" She pointed back toward the mummy.

"Help us!" I screamed.

Nila's green eyes widened in surprise. "What can I do?" she asked. And then her expression changed quickly to anger. "What can I do about you two kids? You shouldn't be here. You're going to ruin everything!"

"Huh?" I cried out in surprise.

Nila stepped into the room. She raised her right hand.

In the dim light, I struggled to make out what she was holding up.

My little mummy hand!

She raised it toward the mummy! "Come to me, my brother!" Nila called.

23

"How did you get my mummy hand? What are you doing?" I demanded.

Nila ignored my questions. She held the flashlight in one hand. She gripped the little hand in the other, holding it up toward the approaching mummy.

"Come here, my brother!" she called, waving the hand, summoning the mummy. "It is I, Princess Nila!"

Its legs cracking, its brittle bones breaking inside the gauze wrappings, the mummy obediently dragged itself forward.

"Nila—stop it! What are you *doing*?" Sari shrieked.

But Nila continued to ignore us. "It is I, your sister!" she called to the mummy. A triumphant smile crossed her pretty face. Her green eyes sparkled like flashing emeralds in the darting light.

"I have waited so long for this day," Nila told

102

the mummy. "I have waited so many centuries, my brother, hoping that someday someone would uncover your tomb and we could be reunited."

Nila's face glowed with excitement. The little mummy hand trembled in her hand. "I have brought you back to life, my brother!" she called to the mummy. "I have waited for centuries. But it will all be worth it. You and I will share all this treasure. And with our powers, we shall rule Egypt together—as we did three thousand years ago!"

She lowered her eyes to me. "Thank you, Gabe!" she cried. "Thank you for the Summoner! As soon as I saw it, I knew I had to have it. I knew it could bring my brother back to me! The ancient words weren't enough. I needed the Summoner, too!"

"Give it back!" I demanded, reaching out for it. "It's mine, Nila. Give it back."

A cruel laugh escaped her throat. "You won't be needing it, Gabe," she said softly.

She waved the hand at the mummy. "Destroy them, my brother!" she ordered. "Destroy them now! There can be no witnesses!"

"Nooo!" Sari shrieked. She and I both dove to the doorway. But Nila moved quickly to block our path.

I shoved my shoulder against her, trying to push her away like a football lineman. But Nila held her ground with surprising strength.

"Nila — let us go!" Sari demanded, breathing hard.

Nila smiled and shook her head. "No witnesses," she murmured.

"Nila — we just want to get Daddy out of here. You can do what you want!" Sari insisted desperately.

Nila ignored her and raised her eyes to the mummy. "Destroy them both!" she called. "They cannot leave this tomb alive!"

Sari and I spun around to see the mummy lumbering toward us. Its blackened skull glowed in the dim light. It trailed long strips of yellowed gauze across the dirt floor as it dragged itself closer.

Closer.

I turned back to the door. Nila blocked the way. My eyes darted frantically around the chamber.

No way to escape.

No escape.

The mummy lurched toward Sari and me.

And reached out its cold, cold hands to obey Nila's cruel command.

Sari and I darted toward the door. But Nila blocked our escape.

Its vacant eyes gazing blindly at us, its jaw frozen in a hideous skeletal grin, the mummy hurtled toward us.

Raised its arms stiffly.

Stretched out its hands.

Dove at us with a final, desperate lurch.

And to my shock, reached past Sari and me — and wrapped its tarred hands around Nila's throat.

Her mouth opened in a choked cry of protest.

The mummy tilted back its head as it gripped her. Its tarred lips moved, and a dry cough cut through the air. And then the whispered words, dry as death, escaped the mummy's throat:

"Let me . . . rest in peace!"

Nila uttered another choked cry.

The mummy tightened its fierce grip on her throat.

I spun around and grabbed its arm. "Let her go!" I screamed.

A dry wheeze erupted from the blackened skull. Its hands tightened around Nila, bending her back, bending her toward the floor.

Nila's eyes shut in defeat. Her hands flew up helplessly. The flashlight and the mummy hand fell to the floor.

I grabbed my little mummy hand and shoved it into my jeans pocket. "Let go! Let go! Let go!" I shrieked. I leaped onto the mummy's back and tried to pull its hands from Nila's throat.

It let out a defiant roar, a harsh whisper of anger.

Then it heaved itself up straight and struggled to toss me off its shoulders.

I gasped, startled by the mummy's surprising strength.

As I started to slide off the mummy's bandaged back, I reached out my hand, grabbing desperately, grabbing air, trying not to fall.

My hand grabbed on to Nila's amber pendant.

"Hey!" I cried out as the mummy gave a hard toss.

I tumbled off.

The pendant tore off its chain. It fell from my hand, crashed to the floor—and shattered.

"Nooooooooooo!" Nila's horrified wail shook the walls.

The mummy froze.

Nila spun out of the mummy's grasp. Backed away. Her eyes wide with terror. "My life! My *life!*" she shrieked.

She bent and struggled to pick up shards of amber from the floor. But the pendant had shattered into a hundred tiny pieces.

"My life!" Nila wailed, staring at the smooth pieces in her palm. She raised her eyes to Sari and me. "I lived inside the pendant!" she cried. "At night, I crept inside. It kept me alive for over three thousand years! And now . . . now . . . ohhhhh . . ."

As her voice trailed off, Nila began to shrink.

Her head, her arms, her entire body grew tinier . . . tinier . . . until she disappeared into her clothes.

And a few seconds later, as Sari and I gaped down in horror and shock, a black scarab crawled out from under the sweatshirt and jeans. The scarab moved unsteadily at first. Then it quickly scuttled away over the dirt floor, disappearing into the darkness.

"That—that beetle—" Sari stammered. "Is it Nila?"

I nodded. "I guess," I said, staring down at Nila's crumpled clothes.

"Do you think she was really an ancient Egyptian princess? Prince Khor-Ru's sister?" Sari murmured.

"It's all so weird," I replied. I was thinking hard,

trying to piece it all together, trying to make sense of what Nila had said.

"She must have returned to her scarab form every night," I told Sari, thinking out loud. "She crawled into the amber and slept inside it. It kept her alive—until . . ."

"Until you smashed the amber pendant," Sari whispered.

"Yes." I nodded. "It was an accident—" I started.

But I choked on my words as I felt a cold hand close on my shoulder.

And knew that the mummy had grabbed me from behind.

The hand rested on my shoulder. The cold seeped through my T-shirt. "Let go!" I screamed.

I spun around—and my heart skipped a beat. "Uncle Ben!" I cried.

"Daddy!" Sari leaped forward and threw her arms around him. "Daddy—you're okay!"

He pulled his hand off my shoulder and rubbed the back of his head. He blinked his eyes uncertainly and shook his head, still a little dazed.

Behind him, I saw the mummy standing hunched over, frozen. Lifeless once again.

"Whew. I'm still groggy," Uncle Ben said, sweeping a hand back through his thick black hair. "What a close call."

"It's all my fault," I admitted. "I repeated the words five times, Uncle Ben. I didn't mean to bring the mummy back to life, but—"

A smile crossed my uncle's face. He lowered his arm around my shoulders. "You didn't do it, Gabe," he said softly. "Nila got there first."

He sighed. "I didn't believe in the power of the chant," he said softly. "But I do now. Nila stole your mummy hand and chanted the ancient words. She used the Summoner to bring the mummy to life. Dr. Fielding and I were both suspicious of her."

"You were?" I cried, surprised. "But I thought—"

"I became suspicious of Nila at dinner," Uncle Ben explained. "Remember? She asked me what were the *six* ancient words to bring the dead to life? Well, I had never revealed that there were six. So I wondered how Nila knew there were six words."

Uncle Ben put an arm around Sari's shoulders, too, and led us to the wall. Then he leaned his back against the wall, rubbing the back of his head.

"That's why I hurried to the communications tent right after dinner," Uncle Ben continued. "I phoned the Cairo *Sun*. They had never heard of Nila at the newspaper. So I knew she was a fake."

"But we saw Dr. Fielding pull you from the tent," Sari broke in. "We saw him force you into the pyramid, and—"

Uncle Ben chuckled. "You two aren't very good spies," he scolded. "Dr. Fielding didn't force me to do anything. He had spotted Nila sneaking into the pyramid. So he found me at the

110

communications tent. And the two of us hurried to the pyramid to see what Nila was up to.

"We got there too late," Uncle Ben continued. "She had already brought the mummy to life. Dr. Fielding and I tried to stop her. She hit me over the head with her flashlight. She dragged me to the mummy case. I guess she stuffed me inside."

He rubbed his head. "That's all I remember. Until now. Until I awoke and saw Nila turn into a scarab."

"We saw Dr. Fielding hurry out of the pyramid," Sari reported. "He walked right past me. He had the weirdest look on his face, and—"

She stopped and her mouth dropped open. We all heard the sounds at the same time.

The scraping of feet on the floor outside the burial chamber.

My heart jumped to my throat. I grabbed Uncle Ben's arm.

The footsteps dragged closer.

More mummies.

More mummies brought to life, staggering toward the prince's tomb.

I reached into my jeans pocket for my little mummy hand. Pressing my back against the wall, I raised my eyes to the chamber doorway—and waited.

Waited for the mummies to appear.

But to my surprise, Dr. Fielding burst into the room, followed by four dark-uniformed police officers, hands at their gun holsters.

"Ben—are you okay?" Dr. Fielding called to my uncle. "Where is the young woman?"

"She . . . escaped," Uncle Ben told him.

How could he explain that she had turned into a bug?

The police explored the chamber warily. Their eyes came to rest on the mummy, frozen in place near the doorway.

"I'm so glad you're okay, Ben," Dr. Fielding said, placing a hand warmly on Uncle Ben's shoulder. Then he turned to Sari. "I'm afraid I owe you an apology, Sari," he said, frowning.

"When I ran out of here, I must have been in shock. I remember seeing you outside the pyramid. But I don't remember saying anything to you."

"That's okay," Sari replied quietly.

"I'm really sorry if I frightened you," Dr. Fielding told her. "Your dad had been knocked unconscious by that crazy young woman. And all I could think about was calling the police as fast as possible."

"Well, the excitement is over," Uncle Ben said, smiling. "Let's all get out of here."

We started toward the doorway, but a police officer interrupted. "Could I just ask one question?" he asked, staring at the upright mummy in the center of the floor. "Did that mummy walk?"

"Of course not!" Uncle Ben replied quickly, a grin spreading over his face. "If it could walk, what would it be doing in *this* dump?"

Well, once again, I turned out to be the hero of the day. And, of course, later in the tent, I wasted no time in bragging about my courage to Sari.

Sari had no choice. She had to sit there and take it. After all, *I* was the one who had stopped the mummy and turned Nila back into a beetle by smashing her pendant.

"At least you're not too conceited!" Sari shot back, rolling her eyes.

Lame. Really lame.

113

"Well, that scarab crawled away and disappeared," she said. An evil smile crossed Sari's lips. "I'll bet that bug is waiting for you, Gabe. I'll bet it's waiting for you in your cot, waiting to bite you."

I laughed. "Sari, you'd say anything to try to scare me. You just can't stand the idea that *I'm* the hero!"

"You're right," she replied dryly. "I *can't* stand the idea. Good night, Gabe."

A few minutes later, I was in my pajamas and ready for bed. What a night! What an amazing night!

As I slid into the cot and pulled up the covers, I knew it was a night I would never forget.

"Ouch!"

BEHIND THE SCREAMS

RETURN OF THE MUMMY

CONTENTS

Bonus material written and compiled
by Gabrielle S. Balkan

About the Author

R.L. Stine's books are read all over the world. So far, his books have sold more than 300 million copies, making him one of the most popular children's authors in history. Besides Goosebumps, R.L. Stine has written the teen series Fear Street, the funny series Rotten School, as well as the Mostly Ghostly series, The Nightmare Room series, and the two-book thriller *Dangerous Girls*. R.L. Stine lives in New York with his wife, Jane, and Minnie, his King Charles spaniel. You can learn more about him at www.RLStine.com.

Q & A with R.L. Stine

Return of the Mummy, like *Revenge of the Living Dummy* and *Creep from the Deep*, is a follow-up to an earlier Goosebumps book. How do you decide which books will have a scary sequel? Do you think any of your other books are begging for a creepy companion?

R.L. Stine (RLS): *The ocean is vast and huge and holds untold mysteries. I guess I could write a hundred sequels to* Deep Trouble. *And everyone loves Slappy the dummy—he's so rude and evil. So I've written a bunch of Slappy books. Recently, I've been thinking of writing a sequel to the very first Goosebumps book—* Welcome to Dead House. *That was actually a zombie book, and these days zombies are very popular. Which book do you think I should write a sequel to?*

Have you ever been to Egypt? Would you like to go?

RLS: *I've written so many books about Egypt and mummies and the pyramids. But I've never traveled there. I would love to go. I think it would be fascinating, especially after writing about it so often. Whenever I think about going, something comes up, and I have to cancel. I guess you could call it Curse of the Egyptian Travel Plans.*

Do you base any of your characters on people you have known?

RLS: *Not very often. When my son was in school, I used a lot of his friends' names in the books. In fact, I had his school directory—and just about every kid in his school was in a Goosebumps book! But I usually like to make up my characters' personalities from my imagination. It's more fun that way.*

Do you ever have trouble coming up with what your characters will do next? If so, what do you do?

RLS: *I spend a lot of time plotting each book before I start to write. I do a chapter-by-chapter outline of all the action—everything that happens in the book. This is where I do all my thinking. So when I start to write the book, I don't have to think about what my characters will do next. I already know what they are going to do!*

Would you ever want to write a book with another author?

RLS: *Yes. I would love to get ALL the scary authors in the US together, and we'd all work on one book. That book would be the scariest in history—no reader would survive it!*

The next Goosebumps HorrorLand is called *The Horror at Chiller House*. What kind of terrifying adventure can we expect in the conclusion of the Jonathan Chiller saga?

RLS: *Well, six kids suddenly find themselves back in Chiller's souvenir store at HorrorLand. How did they get there? Why were they pulled back? Jonathan Chiller turns out to be a very weird dude. He likes to make up games. He brought the kids back to play a game he thought up. I'll give you a hint about the game: It involves crossbows. Yes, the game is dangerous and deadly. And the six kids find themselves in a terrifying adventure. This may be the scariest HorrorLand book I've written.*

To find out whether R.L. Stine likes to garden, check out the special collector's edition of
REVENGE OF THE LAWN GNOMES.

TOP TEN TOMB JOBS

Dying was a big business in ancient Egypt. From embalmer to professional mourner, these were the top ten weirdest ways to make a paycheck in the tomb.

1. EMBALMER

If your pediatrician traveled back in time to visit with Queen Cleopatra in the first century B.C., the doc might have been an embalmer, a job for the highly trained and highly respected. Instead of wearing a white coat and stethoscope, he'd put on a mask of Anubis, the god of embalming, while he worked.

2. CUTTER

On the opposite end of the job spectrum was the cutter: a lowly profession usually confined to **CRIMINALS** or people who couldn't find other, more respectable work. The cutter made incisions in the body so the lungs, liver, stomach, and intestines could be removed. Even though the job needed to be done, people often cursed and stoned the cutters.

3. MUMMY MASK MAKER

If you've always been fascinated by papier-mâché piñatas, you might be interested in a job as a mummy mask maker. It was an important job because the mask helped the dead person be recognized in the afterlife. Ritzy types, like members of royalty, had masks made from gold and decorated with jewels.

4. MUMMY CASE MAKER

Doodlers would be good candidates for the mummy case maker because the mummy case was decorated with **HIEROGLYPHIC** messages to help the mummy on its journey into the afterlife. The mummy case was made from old papyrus, which dried into the shape of the body. The case went inside the coffin, made by—you guessed it—the

5. COFFIN MAKER

As far as coffins went, ancient Egyptians thought two dead beds where better than one. In fact, royalty were buried in several cedar coffins that fit one inside the other. Like with all things mummy, the richer the client, the fancier the coffin. The coffins of top customers were inlaid with gold and jewels.

6. SARCOPHAGUS MAKER

After the paperlike case and a couple of wooden coffins came the stone sarcophagus. And just like the other items, this part of the mummification process involved high artistry: The sarcophagus was carved with pictures and hieroglyphs inside and out.

7. SHABTI

Another job you'd want to stay away from: Shabti were figurines placed in tombs to do all the dirty work in the afterlife—they were like servants for the dead. Though you wouldn't want to BE a shabti, making them could be a lot of fun.

8. MOURNER

Calling all drama queens and theater stars! This long-term job lasted from death until **BURIAL**—that's more than 70 days! You'd need to bring friends on the interview, because the wealthy hired lots of people to moan, wail, and pound on their chests.

9. TOMB ROBBER

This may be the hardest job yet because tombs were NOT easy to get into. Plus, tomb robbers had to unmummify a mummy to get to the jewelry! If you failed at this job you wouldn't get fired. Instead, you'd get beaten with a cane, branded with a hot iron, and sent to work in mines, usually after having your nose or hand cut off.

10. POLICE

The tomb police didn't worry much about collecting evidence to bring to court because they got to punish lawbreakers on the spot. Usually with a big stick.

MUMMY MATCHUP

Sure, you may know how to remove a mummy's brain with a hook, but can you correctly answer these Goosebumps mummy questions?

1. Abby and Peter discover a room full of half-living mummies in which book?

    a. THE CURSE OF THE MUMMY'S TOMB
    b. THE MUMMY AT THE DOOR
    c. GOOSEBUMPS HORRORLAND: WHO'S YOUR MUMMY?

2. Where does THE CURSE OF THE MUMMY'S TOMB take place?

    a. Alexandria
    b. Vermont
    c. Cairo

3. Gabe gets trapped in an underground chamber full of scorpions in which book?

    a. THE CURSE OF THE MUMMY'S TOMB
    b. RETURN OF THE MUMMY
    c. GOOSEBUMPS HORRORLAND: WHO'S YOUR MUMMY?

4. What does Abby have that Tuttan-Rha wants in GOOSEBUMPS HORRORLAND: WHO'S YOUR MUMMY?

    a. Liver

    b. Hair

    c. Blood

5. Uncle Ben is forced into a stone mummy case in which book?

    a. WELCOME TO THE MUMMY'S TOMB

    b. RETURN OF THE MUMMY

    c. GOOSEBUMPS HORRORLAND: MUMMY GOT YOUR TONGUE?

6. What happens to Nila at the end of RETURN OF THE MUMMY?

    a. She turns into a scarab beetle.

    b. She is choked by a mummy.

    c. She marries Uncle Ben.

7. What is supposed to happen when Granny Vee eats the liver from Tuttan-Rha's house?

    a. She will not be hungry.

    b. She will die.

    c. She will live forever.

8. What does Ahmed try to do to Gabe and Sari?

   a. Kidnap them
   b. Throw them in a tar pit
   c. Embalm them for mummification

9. What did Nila steal from Gabe?

   a. A mummy hand
   b. An amber necklace
   c. An ancient amulet

10. Which mummy book did R.L. Stine write first?

   a. **THE CURSE OF THE MUMMY'S TOMB**
   b. **RETURN OF THE MUMMY**
   c. **GOOSEBUMPS HORRORLAND: WHO'S YOUR MUMMY?**

HOW MUCH IS THAT SCARAB IN THE WINDOW?

If you were an animal lover in ancient Egypt, you'd know all the habits of these strange creatures, both real and unreal.

ANUBIS

This **JACKAL-HEADED** god was very important to the dead; he helped with the burial and the difficult transition into the afterlife. Some say his name means "to rot," while others go with the more pleasant-sounding "king's son."

APEP, *also known as* APOPHIS, THE DESTROYER

Not just any old garden snake, Apep was thought to be a demon from the underworld who battled against the sun god, Ra, in the form of a 48-foot water serpent—that's nearly as wide as a basketball court! In Apep's battles against Ra, the evil god was thought to eat the sun each night.

KEPHRI

A major god whose name means "to come into being" is associated with the real-life dung beetle, a type of scarab beetle. Since scarab beetles lay their eggs in the bodies of **DEAD ANIMALS**, ancient Egyptians believed they were created from dead matter. Rather than be creeped out by this, they instead connected Kephri with rebirth, renewal, and resurrection.

TAWERET

This goddess, called "she who is great," had a hippopotamus head, lion limbs, and a big belly, and was a fierce protector of pregnant women and babies.

DRESS LIKE AN EGYPTIAN

Thanks to lice infestations, bad hair days were common along the Nile. But since baseball caps were still thousands of years away, our friends in ancient Egypt had to come up with a few other tricks.

COLOR

Here's a hair dye you won't find in your local drug store: Women sometimes enhanced their natural hair color with a mixture of oil and **BOILED BLOOD**.

WIG

Whether they shaved their heads or cut their hair short, both men and women were happy with wigs. The wigs never turned gray, and thanks to small risers underneath, which allowed for a nice breeze on the scalp, were perfect for hot days, of which there were many!

SCENTED CONE

Have any extra lard on hand? If so you are halfway to making your very own scented hair cone, which is just the thing to put atop your head on the way to an ancient Egyptian party. With the scented hair cone in place, ladies and gentlemen merely waited for the mixture of perfumed oil and wax or rendered animal fat to melt and release the wonderful scent. It was like a time-release air freshener for the head!

Add more Goosebumps to your collection!
Here's a chilling preview of

Goosebumps HorrorLand™

THE HORROR AT CHILLER HOUSE

The adventure continues in the world's scariest theme park!

5

"Whoa." I uttered a startled cry.

White light quivered all around me, so bright I still saw it when I shut my eyes.

Slowly, the light faded. I blinked a few times. I shook my head. Ran my hand through my blond hair.

Sometimes you see funny videos of people spinning around inside big clothes dryers. That's what I thought of. That's what I felt like.

Like I'd been spinning endlessly in burning hot air.

And now the room started to come into focus. I saw cluttered shelves and tall display cases. A grinning skeleton propped against the back door.

I knew where I was. This was the little souvenir store where I bought that evil dummy, Slappy. I was back in Chiller House. Back in HorrorLand.

But — how?

I shook myself hard, as if trying to wake from a dream. *Am I going crazy?*

That thought flashed through my spinning brain.

I reviewed the facts. I had to make everything clear.

My name. It's Ray Gordon. I'm twelve. My little brother's name is Brandon. I shouldn't call him *little* brother. He's twice my size.

Okay. My memory was fine. My brain wasn't totally playing jokes on me.

But one minute I had been at home in my room. And now here I stood, in the aisle of this little shop in HorrorLand.

And as the bright light faded and my mind cleared, I realized I wasn't alone. I saw other kids about my age huddled together at the front of the store. I counted them. Five in all. Three boys and two girls.

They all stared at me, as if they'd been waiting for me. But their faces were filled with surprise.

I took a few shaky steps toward them. "Are you — are you surprised to be here, too?" I stammered.

They all began talking at once. I could tell they were as confused as me. Confused and frightened.

I gazed around. The six of us were alone in the store. Where was Jonathan Chiller, the old guy who owned the place?

I suddenly remembered. "I held a tiny Horror in my hand," I said. "It was glowing. Green and yellow light came out of it, and it pulled me . . ."

"Me, too," the girl with curly red hair said.

"The little Horrors brought us here somehow," a round-faced boy, built like a middle linebacker, chimed in.

"Were you all here in this store before?" I asked.

Everyone nodded and said yes.

"Did you all take something home from here?" I asked.

Again, the answer was yes.

"I picked a joke coin," the very tall girl with straight brown hair and shiny blue eyes said. "A two-headed coin. It got me in all kinds of trouble."

That started everyone talking again.

"I bought a leather cord with an ancient dog tooth on it," the big, round-faced boy said.

"I brought home Insta-Gro Pets that grew gigantic!"

Everyone had a crazy story. I think I had the craziest of all. Who would believe a wooden ventriloquist's dummy could come to life?

As we all shared our stories of horror, I began to catch their names. The middle linebacker with the very worried expression was Andy. The way-tall girl was Jessica. The other girl, the one with red hair, was Meg.

Marco was the one who talked about comic books and some superhero character named The Ooze. Marco was tall and dark and serious looking.

The other boy was Sam. He was short and smaller than the rest of us. He had black hair and dark eyes. His two front teeth poked out when he talked, like Bugs Bunny teeth.

It didn't take long to put the stories together. All six of us had bought gifts or souvenirs here. All six of us had scary adventures, mostly because of those souvenirs.

"The old dude, Jonathan Chiller, gave me a little Horror," Sam said. "He told me to take a little Horror home with me."

"Me, too!" several kids cried.

We all started talking again. It turned out that Chiller didn't let any of us pay for our gifts. He said we could pay him *next time*.

I felt a chill run slowly down my back. I suddenly felt cold all over.

Is this it? Is this payback time?

The shelves and cases were jammed with items. Big stuffed monsters had tumbled out into the aisle. I saw a headless monkey with a lightbulb where its head should be.

Grinning, prune-wrinkled shrunken heads dangled on rubber cords from the ceiling. Globs of rubber vomit glistened wetly on a low shelf. One glass case was jammed full with ugly plastic cockroaches.

The stuff all seemed really funny the first time I was here with my brother. But now it was just frightening.

"How do we get home?" Meg asked. "My parents must be frantic."

"Does anyone have a phone?" I asked.

Sam pulled a cell phone from his jeans pocket. He peered at the screen. He pushed the power button. He shook the phone.

Then he let out a sigh. "Totally dead. I don't

get it. I just recharged it before . . . before I was brought here."

No one else had a phone with them. We had all been pulled away from our homes without any warning.

"Where is Chiller?" I said. "We have a lot of questions for him."

I made my way to the back room. The door had a werewolf poster across it. It swung open easily. I poked my head inside.

A tiny supply room. More shelves of weird stuff. But no sign of the old shop owner.

We all walked up and down the aisles. He wasn't hiding anywhere in the store.

"This is kind of like a comic book story," Marco said. "You know. Time travel. No, not time travel. But some kind of travel. There was an Ooze story about a bunch of kids who could jump from one place to another."

"But this isn't a comic book," Meg said, shaking her head. "This is our *lives*."

I stepped behind the front desk. The screen saver was on the computer monitor. It showed skeleton fish swimming in black water.

I saw a stack of papers in the corner of the desk. I picked them up.

"Hey. This is *disturbing*," I said.

I held up the stack. They were photographs. I turned them around and shuffled through them. Grainy, blurred black-and-white photos.

"That's *us*!" Sam said. He grabbed some of the photos from my hand and studied them. "Photos taken of each of us in this store."

Jessica pointed up to the ceiling. We all saw the small black security camera up there. It was aimed down at the front desk.

"Chiller took our picture when we stood here," Sam said.

I took the photos back from him. My picture was on the top. I gazed at it — and felt a chill.

"Look," I said. I held it up so everyone could see it. "Someone has added something to it."

Yes. Someone had taken a black marker. They drew an arrow through my head.

I shuffled through the stack. Jessica's picture had an arrow drawn through her head, too. And Meg's. And Andy's.

"All of them," I said. "Did Chiller do this? Someone very carefully drew an arrow through our heads."

"Creepy," Andy muttered. "What does it mean? Is it some kind of sick threat?"

I heard a loud cough. We all turned toward the front door.

Jonathan Chiller stood in the doorway. Blue light from the front window poured over him, making him look ghostlike.

"Welcome back," he said, and a cold smile spread slowly over his face.

Even more frights to keep you awake
at night! Here's a preview of

REVENGE OF THE LAWN GNOMES

Another classic Goosebumps adventure
with brand-new bonus material

Clack, Clack, Clack.

The Ping-Pong ball clattered over the basement floor. "Yes!" I cried as I watched Mindy chase after it.

It was a hot, sticky June afternoon. The first Monday of summer vacation. And Joe Burton had just made another excellent shot.

That's me. Joe Burton. I'm twelve. And there is nothing I love better than slamming the ball in my older sister's face and making her chase after it.

I'm not a bad sport. I just like to show Mindy that she's not as great as she thinks she is.

You might guess that Mindy and I do not always agree on things. The fact is, I'm really not like anyone else in my family.

Mindy, Mom, and Dad are all blond, skinny, and tall. I have brown hair. And I'm kind of pudgy and short. Mom says I haven't had my growth spurt yet.

So I'm a shrimp. And it's hard for me to see over the Ping-Pong net. But I can still beat Mindy with one hand tied behind my back.

As much as I love to win, Mindy hates to lose. And she doesn't play fair at all. Every time I make a great move, she says it doesn't count.

"Joe, *kicking* the ball over the net is not legal," she whined as she scooped out the ball from under the couch.

"Give me a break!" I cried. "All the Ping-Pong champions do it. They call it the Soccer Slam."

Mindy rolled her huge green eyes. "Oh, puh-lease!" she muttered. "My serve."

Mindy is weird. She's probably the weirdest fourteen-year-old in town.

Why? I'll tell you why.

Take her room. Mindy arranges all her books in alphabetical order — by author. Do you believe it?

And she fills out a card for each one. She files them in the top drawer of her desk. Her own private card catalog.

If she could, she'd probably cut the tops off the books so they'd all be the same size.

She is *so* organized. Her closet is organized by color. All the reds come first. Then the oranges. Then the yellows. Then come the greens, blues, and purples. She hangs her clothes in the same order as the rainbow.

And at dinner, she eats around her plate clockwise. Really! I've watched her. First her mashed potatoes. Then all her peas. And then her meat loaf. If she finds one pea in her mashed potatoes, she totally loses it!

Weird. Really weird.

Me? I'm not organized. I'm cool. I'm not serious like my sister. I can be pretty funny. My friends think I'm a riot. Everyone does. Except Mindy.

"Come on, serve already," I called out. "Before the end of the century."

Mindy stood on her side of the table, carefully lining up her shot. She stands in exactly the same place every time. With her feet exactly the same space apart. Her footprints are worn into the carpet.

"Ten–eight and serving," Mindy finally called out. She always calls out the score before she serves. Then she swung her arm back.

I held the paddle up to my mouth like a microphone. "She pulls her arm back," I announced. "The crowd is hushed. It's a tense moment."

"Joe, stop acting like a jerk," she snapped. "I have to concentrate."

I love pretending I'm a sports announcer. It drives Mindy nuts.

Mindy pulled her arm back again. She tossed the Ping-Pong ball up into the air. And . . .

"A spider!" I screamed. "On your shoulder!"

"*Yaaaiiii!*" Mindy dropped the paddle and began slapping her shoulder furiously. The ball clattered onto the table.

"Gotcha!" I cried. "My point."

"No way!" Mindy shouted angrily. "You're just a cheater, Joe." She smoothed the shoulders of her pink T-shirt carefully. She picked up the ball and swatted it over the net.

"At least I'm a *funny* cheater!" I replied. I twirled around in a complete circle and belted the ball. It bounced once on my side before sailing over the net.

"Foul," Mindy announced. "You're always fouling."

I waved my paddle at her. "Get a life," I said. "It's a game. It's supposed to be fun."

"I'm beating you," Mindy replied. "That's fun."

I shrugged. "Who cares? Winning isn't everything."

"Where did you read that?" she asked. "In a bubble gum comic?" Then she rolled her eyes again. I think someday her eyes are going to roll right out of her head!

I rolled my eyes, too — back into my head until only the whites showed. "Neat trick, huh?"

"Cute, Joe," Mindy muttered. "Really cute. You'd better watch out. One day your eyes might not come back down. Which would be an improvement!"

"Lame joke," I replied. "Very lame."

Mindy lined up her feet carefully again.

"She's in her serve position," I spoke into my paddle. "She's nervous. She's . . ."

"Joe!" Mindy whined. "Quit it!"

She tossed the Ping-Pong ball into the air. She swung the paddle, and —

"Gross!" I shouted. "What's that big green glob hanging out of your nose?"

Mindy ignored me this time. She tapped the ball over the net.

I dove forward and whacked it with the tip of my paddle. It spun high over the net and landed in the corner of the basement. Between the washing machine and the dryer.

Mindy jogged after the ball on her long, thin legs. "Hey, where's Buster?" she called out. "Wasn't he sleeping next to the dryer?"

Buster is our dog. A giant black Rottweiler with a head the size of a basketball. He loves snoozing on the old sleeping bag we keep in the corner of the basement. Especially when we're down here playing Ping-Pong.

Everyone is afraid of Buster. For about three seconds. Then he starts licking them with his long, wet tongue. Or rolls onto his back and begs to have his belly scratched.

"Where is he, Joe?" Mindy bit her lip.

"He's around here somewhere," I replied. "Why

are you always worrying about Buster? He weighs over a hundred pounds. He can take care of himself."

Mindy frowned. "Not if Mr. McCall catches him. Remember what he said the last time Buster chomped on his tomato plants?"

Mr. McCall is our next-door neighbor. Buster loves the McCalls' yard. He likes to nap under their huge, shady elm tree.

And dig little holes all over their lawn. And sometimes big holes.

And snack in their vegetable garden.

Last year, Buster dug up every head of Mr. McCall's lettuce. And ate his biggest zucchini plant for dessert.

I guess that's why Mr. McCall hates Buster. He said the next time he catches him in his garden, he's going to turn him into fertilizer.

My dad and Mr. McCall are the two best gardeners in town. They're nuts about gardening. Totally nuts.

I think working in a garden is kind of fun, too. But I don't let that get around. My friends think gardening is for nerds.

Dad and Mr. McCall are always battling it out at the annual garden show. Mr. McCall usually takes first place. But last year, Dad and I won the blue ribbon for our tomatoes.

That drove Mr. McCall crazy. When Dad's name

was announced, Mr. McCall's face turned as red as our tomatoes.

So Mr. McCall is desperate to win this year. He started stocking up on plant food and bug spray months ago.

And he planted something that nobody else in North Bay grows. Strange orange-green melons called casabas.

Dad says that Mr. McCall has made a big mistake. He says that casabas will never grow any bigger than tennis balls. The growing season in Minnesota is too short.

"McCall's garden loses," I declared. "Our tomatoes are definitely going to win again this year. And thanks to my special soil, they'll grow as big as beach balls!"

"So will your head," Mindy shot back.

I stuck out my tongue and crossed my eyes. It seemed like a good reply.

"Whose serve is it?" I asked. Mindy was taking so long, I lost track.

"It's still my serve," she replied, carefully placing her feet.

We were interrupted by footsteps. Heavy, booming footsteps on the stairs behind Mindy.

"Who is that?" Mindy cried.

And then he appeared behind her. And my eyes nearly bulged right out of my head.

"Oh, no!" I screamed. "It's . . . McCall!"

Catch the MOST WANTED Goosebumps® villain. UNDEAD OR ALIVE!

NOW A MAJOR
MOTION PICTURE

JACK BLACK

Goosebumps

The Original Bone-Chilling Series

—with Exclusive Author Interviews!

R. L. Stine's Fright Fest!
Now with Splat Stats and More!

REVENGE OF THE LIVING DUMMY
R.L. STINE

CREEP FROM THE DEEP
R.L. STINE

MONSTER BLOOD FOR BREAKFAST!
R.L. STINE

THE SCREAM OF THE HAUNTED MASK
R.L. STINE

DR. MANIAC VS. ROBBY SCHWARTZ
R.L. STINE

WHO'S YOUR MUMMY?
R.L. STINE

MY FRIENDS CALL ME MONSTER
R.L. STINE

SAY CHEESE - AND DIE SCREAMING!
R.L. STINE

WELCOME TO CAMP SLITHER
R.L. STINE

THE SCARIEST PLACE ON EARTH!

HELP! WE HAVE STRANGE POWERS!
R.L. STINE

ESCAPE FROM HORRORLAND
R.L. STINE

THE STREETS OF PANIC PARK
R.L. STINE

WHEN THE GHOST DOG HOWLS
R.L. STINE

LITTLE SHOP OF HAMSTERS
R.L. STINE

HEADS, YOU LOSE!
R.L. STINE

WEIRDO HALLOWEEN
R.L. STINE

THE WIZARD OF OOZE
R.L. STINE

SLAPPY NEW YEAR!
R.L. STINE

THE HORROR AT CHILLER HOUSE
R.L. STINE

SCHOLASTIC

www.EnterHorrorLand.com

GBHL19B

GOOSEBUMPS HALL OF HORRORS

THERE'S ALWAYS ROOM FOR ONE MORE SCREAM!

An all-new series from fright-master R.L. Stine!

CLAWS!
R.L. STINE

NIGHT OF THE GIANT EVERYTHING
R.L. STINE

THE FIVE MASKS OF DR. SCREEM
R.L. STINE

WHY I QUIT ZOMBIE SCHOOL
R.L. STINE

DON'T SCREAM!
R.L. STINE

THE BIRTHDAY PARTY OF NO RETURN!
R.L. STINE

■ SCHOLASTIC

www.scholastic.com/goosebumps

GBHOHG